SMALL TOWNS, BIG STORIES

Books by Ruskin Bond

Fiction

Tales of Fosterganj
A Gathering of Friends
Upon an Old Wall Dreaming
The Room on the Roof & Vagrants in the Valley
The Night Train at Deoli and Other Stories
Time Stops at Shamli and Other Stories
Our Trees Still Grow in Dehra
A Season of Ghosts
When Darkness Falls and Other Stories
A Flight of Pigeons
Delhi is Not Far
A Face in the Dark and Other Hauntings
The Sensualist
A Handful of Nuts
Maharani
Secrets

Non-fiction

Rain in the Mountains
Scenes from a Writer's Life
A Book of Simple Living
Love among the Bookshelves
Landour Days
Notes from a Small Room
The India I Love

Anthologies

Classic Ruskin Bond: Complete and Unabridged
Classic Ruskin Bond Volume 2: The Memoirs
Dust on the Mountain: Collected Stories
The Best of Ruskin Bond
Friends in Small Places
Indian Ghost Stories (ed.)
Indian Railway Stories (ed.)
Ghost Stories from the Raj
Tales of the Open Road
Ruskin Bond's Book of Nature
Ruskin Bond's Book of Humour
A Town Called Dehra
The Writer on the Hill

Poetry

Ruskin Bond's Book of Verse
Hip-Hop Nature Boy & Other Poems

SMALL TOWNS, BIG STORIES

NEW & SELECTED FICTION

RUSKIN BOND

ALEPH BOOK COMPANY
An independent publishing firm
promoted by *Rupa Publications India*

First published in India in 2017
by Aleph Book Company
7/16 Ansari Road, Daryaganj
New Delhi 110 002

Copyright © Ruskin Bond 2017

All rights reserved.

The author has asserted his moral rights.

Acknowledgements on Page 190 constitute an extension of the copyright page.

This is a work of fiction. Names, characters, places and incidents are either the product of the author's imagination or are used fictitiously and any resemblance to any actual persons, living or dead, events or locales is entirely coincidental.

No part of this publication may be reproduced, transmitted, or stored in a retrieval system, in any form or by any means, without permission in writing from Aleph Book Company.

ISBN: 978-93-82277-54-5

12 13 14 15

Printed in India

This book is sold subject to the condition that it shall not, by way of trade or otherwise, be lent, resold, hired out, or otherwise circulated without the publisher's prior consent in any form of binding or cover other than that in which it is published.

To
Beena and Rakesh in gratitude
for looking after the most impractical man in the world
while he wrote these and many other stories
in their small flat on the heights of Landour

CONTENTS

Introduction: Small Towns, Big Stories   ix

1. The Big Race   1
2. Up the Spiral Staircase   6
3. A Long Walk for Bina   13
4. When Guavas are Ripe   34
5. The Night Train at Deoli   41
6. The Visitor   46
7. Of Rivers and Pilgrims   51
8. A Good Place for Trees   55
9. Time Stops at Shamli   59
10. Bus Stop, Pipalnagar   95
11. The Funeral   121
12. Some Hill Station Ghosts   125
13. A Hill Station's Vintage Murders   132
14. Kipling's Simla   140
15. Grandfather's Earthquake   146
16. Voting at Barlowganj   151
17. A Magic Oil   159
18. The Tail of the Lizard   164
19. Strychnine in the Cognac   176
20. When the Clock Strikes Thirteen   185
21. The Horseshoe   188

Acknowledgements   190

INTRODUCTION

Small Towns, Big Stories

This collection of what I regard as my finest 'small town' stories, along with some brand new ones, was put together with the help of David Davidar, publisher, editor and friend, who has played an important part in my literary journey—at first with Penguin India and then with Aleph. I was especially happy to be able to include some of my early work—'The Big Race', 'The Visitor', 'The Night Train at Deoli', 'Time Stops at Shamli'—written when I was in my early twenties, freelancing from Dehradun, then a small town of some fifty thousand souls. It is no longer a small town today, over fifty years later, rather it is a small city with a population exceeding ten lakhs! But that, as they say, is another story.

The 1950s was my 'romantic' period, as far as stories went, and 'The Night Train at Deoli' is still one that appeals to the young and romantic. I am often asked if the girl and the station really existed. When I wrote the story I thought I was making up the name, which appealed to me. Later I discovered that there were at least five Deolis in India—one in Rajasthan, one in Maharashtra, one in Orissa, and two in Madhya Pradesh! They are all small towns, but as far as I know, only one has a railway station.

However, my 'Deoli' is really just a place in my mind; it could be a wayside station almost anywhere. And the same with 'Shamli'. The real Shamli is a prosperous little town in the middle of west

UP's sugarcane belt. And you can say the same of 'Pipalnagar'. You can find mine almost anywhere in northern India, going by a different name. Jamnagar, a small town and port on our western seaboard, was very much a part of my childhood. Later, schooldays were spent in Simla and boyhood in the old 'Dehra'. ('Dehradun', freely translated, means 'Rest camp in the dhun, or valley.')

For many years I have lived in Landour and Mussoorie, and the hills and hill stations have given me much to write about, including the new offerings in this collection. 'Fosterganj' is part of the same scene; a relic of our colonial past.

Oddly enough, although I spent three years in London and five in New Delhi, those great cities never gave me much by way of stories. It is easier to know people in small places. Sometimes you can't help knowing them. Like the boy who walks four miles to school; or the elderly gentleman who is up every morning at five o'clock, taking his morning walk (tap-tap-tap, I hear his walking stick below my window); or that busy little woman gathering firewood for the winter; or the man from the nursery who sells me a potted geranium and ends up telling me the story of his life... So many stories waiting to be told! And, as I have discovered, small towns may be smaller than cities, and there may be fewer people living in them, but the stories they provide a writer with are big, they contain worlds upon worlds within them.

There's yet another advantage to writing about small places. You might get writer's block living in Delhi or Mumbai, but in small town India you won't run out of tales to tell. Like it or not, you are a part of the human comedy.

Ruskin Bond

Landour, Mussoorie
November 2016

THE BIG RACE

Dawn crept quietly over the sleeping town. Only a cock was aware of it, and crowed. Koki heard a soft tapping on the windowpane, and immediately sat up in bed. She was ten years old. Her hair fell about her shoulders in a disorderly fashion and there were slight shadows under her dark eyes, but she was wide awake and listening. The tapping was repeated.

Koki got out of bed and tiptoed across to the window and unlatched it. Ranji was standing outside, looking somewhat disgruntled.

'Come on,' he said. 'It's nearly time.'

Koki put her finger to her lips, for she did not want her parents and grandmother to wake up.

'You go and tell Bhim,' she whispered. 'I'll meet you at the maidan.'

Ranji hurried off in the direction of Bhim's house, and Koki turned from the window and went to the dressing table. She combed her hair carelessly and tied it roughly with a ribbon. She was excited and in a hurry, and had slept in her dress, which was very crushed. Now she was ready to leave.

Very quietly, she pulled open a dressing table drawer, and brought out a cardboard box in which were punctured little holes. She opened the lid of the box to see if Rajkumari was all right.

Rajkumari, a dumpy rhino beetle, was asleep on the core of an apple. Koki did not disturb her. She closed the box and barefoot crept out of the house through the back door.

As soon as she was outside, Koki broke into a run. She did

not stop running until she reached the maidan.

On the maidan, the slanting rays of the early morning sun were just beginning to make emeralds of the dewdrops. Later in the day the grass would dry and be prickly to the feet, but now it was cool and soft. A group of boys had gathered at one corner of the maidan, talking excitedly, and among them were Ranji and Bhim, a lanky, bespectacled boy of fourteen. Koki was the only girl among them.

Bhim's beetle was the favourite for the race. It was a large bamboo beetle, with a slim body and long, slender legs, rather like its master's. It was called 2001. Ranji's beetle was a stone carrier with what looked like a very long pair of whiskers. It was appropriately named Moocha. Koki's beetle was not half as big as the other two. Though she did not know how to tell its sex, she was sure it was a female and had called it Rajkumari.

There were only three entries. Strictly speaking, betting wasn't allowed, but the boys made a few quiet bets among themselves. The prize was a giant insect (there was some disagreement as to whether it was a beetle or an outsize cockroach), which was meant to enable the winner to breed larger racing beetles.

There was some confusion when Ranji's Moocha escaped from his box and took a preliminary canter over the grass; but he was soon caught and returned to his enclosure. Moocha appeared to be in good form, in fact he would be tough competition for Bhim's 2001.

The course was about two metres long, the tracks fifteen centimetres wide. The tracks were fenced with strips of cardboard so that the contestants did not get in each other's way or leave the course altogether. They were held at the starting post by another piece of cardboard, which would be placed behind them as soon as the race began—just to make sure that no one backed out.

A little Sikh boy in a yellow pyjama-suit was acting as starter, and he kept blowing his whistle for order and attention. When the onlookers saw that the race was about to begin, they fell silent.

The little Sikh boy then announced the rules of the race—the contestants were not to be touched during the race, or blown at from behind, or enticed forward with bits of food. They could, however, be cheered on as loudly as anyone wished.

Moocha and 2001 were already at the starting post, but Koki was giving Rajkumari a few words of advice. Rajkumari seemed reluctant to leave her apple core and needed to be taken forcibly to the starting post.

There was further delay when Moocha and 2001 got their horns and whiskers entangled. They had to be separated and calmed down before being placed in their respective tracks. The race was about to start.

Koki knelt on the grass, very quiet and serious, looking from Rajkumari to the finishing line and back again. Ranji was biting his fingernails. Bhim's glasses had clouded over, and he had to keep taking them off and wiping them on his shirt. There was a hush amongst the dozen or so spectators.

'Pee-ee-eeep!' The little Sikh boy blew his whistle.

They were off!

Or rather, Moocha and 2001 were off. Rajkumari was still at the starting post, wondering what had happened to her apple core.

Everyone was cheering madly, and Ranji was jumping up and down, and Bhim's glasses had been knocked off. Moocha was going at a spanking rate. 2001 wasn't taking a great deal of interest in the proceedings, but he was moving, and anything could happen in a race like this.

Koki was on the verge of tears. All the coaching she had given Rajkumari seemed to be of no avail. Her beetle was still looking bewildered and hurt.

'Stop sulking,' said Koki. 'I won't keep you if you don't try.'

Then Moocha stopped suddenly, less than a metre from the finishing line. He seemed to be having trouble with his whiskers, and kept twitching them this way and that. 2001 was catching up slowly but surely, and both Ranji and Bhim were shouting themselves hoarse. Nobody paid any attention to Rajkumari, who was considered to be out of the race; but Koki was using all her willpower to get her racer going.

As 2001 approached Moocha, he seemed to sense his rival's trouble and stopped to find out what was the matter. They could not see each other over the cardboard fence, but otherwise appeared to be communicating very well. Ranji and Bhim were becoming quite frantic in their efforts to rally their faltering steeds, and the cheering on all sides was deafening.

Rajkumari, goaded with rage and frustration at having been deprived of her apple core, now took it into her head to make a bid for liberty and new pastures, and rushed forward in great style.

Koki shouted with joy, but the others did not notice the new challenge until Rajkumari had drawn level with her conferring rivals. There was a gasp from the crowd as Rajkumari strode across the finishing line in record time.

Everyone cheered the gallant outsider. Ranji and Bhim very sportingly shook Koki's hand, congratulating her on Rajkumari's victory. The little Sikh boy in the yellow pyjama-suit blew his whistle for silence and presented Koki with her prize.

Koki gazed in rapture at the new beetle—or was it a cockroach? She stroked its back with her thumb. The insect didn't seem to mind. Then, lest Rajkumari should feel jealous, Koki closed the prize box and, picking up her victorious beetle, returned her to the apple core.

The crowd began to break up. Ranji decided that he would trim Moocha's whiskers before the next race, and Bhim thought 2001 was in need of a special diet.

'Just wait till next Sunday,' said Ranji. 'Then watch my Moocha leave the rest of you standing!'

Bhim said nothing. He looked very thoughtful. There were some new training methods which he was going to try out for next time.

Koki walked home, a cardboard box under each arm. Her

thoughts were busy with the future. She would breed beetles (or would they be cockroaches?) until she had a stable of about twenty. Her racers would win every event, both here and in the next town. They might make her famous. Beetle racing would become a national sport!

Meanwhile, she was happy, and Rajkumari was happy on the apple core, and the new insect was just being an insect and did not know and did not care about anything except how to get out of that wretched box.

UP THE SPIRAL STAIRCASE

We lived in an old palace beside a lake. The palace looked a ruin from the outside, but the rooms were cool and comfortable. We lived in one wing, and my father organized a small school in another wing. His pupils were the children of the raja and the raja's relatives. My father had started life in India as a tea planter; but he had been trained as a teacher and the idea of starting a school in a small state facing the Arabian Sea had appealed to him. The pay wasn't much, but we had a palace to live in, the latest 1938 model Hillman to drive about in, and a number of servants. In those days, of course, everyone had servants (although the servants did not have any). Ayah was our own; but the cook, the bearer, the gardener and the bhisti were all provided by the state.

Sometimes I sat in the schoolroom with the other children (who were all much bigger than me), sometimes I remained in the house with Ayah, sometimes I followed the gardener Dukhi about the spacious garden.

Dukhi means 'sad', and though I never could discover if the gardener had anything to feel sad about, the name certainly suited him. He had grown to resemble the drooping weeds that he was always digging up with a tiny spade. I seldom saw him standing up. He always sat on the ground with his knees well up to his chin, and attacked the weeds from this position. He could spend all day on his haunches, moving about the garden simply by shuffling his feet along the grass.

I tried to imitate his posture, sitting down on my heels and putting my knees into my armpits, but could never hold the position for more than five minutes.

Time had no meaning in a large garden, and Dukhi never hurried. Life, for him, was not a matter of one year succeeding another but of five seasons—winter, spring, hot weather, monsoon and autumn—arriving and departing. His seedbeds had always to be in readiness for the coming season, and he did not look any further than the next monsoon. It was impossible to tell his age. He may have been thirty-six or eighty-six. He was either very young for his years or very old for them.

Dukhi loved bright colours, especially reds and yellows. He liked strongly scented flowers, like jasmine and honeysuckle. He couldn't understand my father's preference for the more delicately perfumed petunias and sweet peas. But I shared Dukhi's fondness for the common, bright orange marigold, which is offered in temples and used to make garlands and nosegays. When the garden was bare of all colour, the marigold would still be there, gay and flashy, challenging the sun.

Dukhi was very fond of making nosegays, and I liked to watch him at work. A sunflower formed the centrepiece. It was surrounded by roses, marigolds and oleanders, fringed with green leaves, and bound together with silver thread. The perfume was overpowering. The nosegays were presented to me or my father on special occasions, that is, on birthdays or any party, at moments of arrival or departure, or to guests of my father's who were considered important.

One day I found Dukhi making a nosegay, and said, 'No one is coming today, Dukhi. It isn't even a birthday.'

'It is a birthday, chota sahib,' he said. 'Little sahib' was the title he had given me. It wasn't much of a title compared to raja sahib or diwan sahib or burra sahib but it was nice to have a title at the age of seven.

'Oh,' I said. 'And is there a party, too?'

'No party.'

'What's the use of a birthday without a party? What's the use of a party without presents?'

'This person doesn't like presents—just flowers.'

'Who is it?' I asked, full of curiosity.

'If you want to find out, you can take these flowers to her. She lives right at the top of the far side of the palace. There are twenty-two steps to climb. Remember that, chota sahib. If you take twenty-three steps, you will go over the edge into the lake!'

༄

I started climbing the stairs.

It was a spiral staircase of wrought iron, and it went round and round and up and up, and it made me quite dizzy and tired.

At the top I found myself on a small balcony, which looked out over the lake and another palace, at the crowded town and the distant harbour. I heard a voice, a rather high, musical voice saying (in English), 'Are you a ghost?' I turned to see who had spoken but found the balcony empty. The voice had come from a dark room.

I turned to the stairway, ready to flee, but the voice said, 'Oh, don't go, there's nothing to be frightened of!'

And so I stood still, peering cautiously into the darkness of the room.

'First tell me—are you a ghost?'

'I'm a boy,' I said.

'And I'm a girl. We can be friends. I can't come out there, so you had better come in. Come along, I'm not a ghost either—not yet, anyway!'

As there was nothing very frightening about the voice, I stepped into the room. It was dark inside, and, coming in from the glare, it took me some time to make out the tiny, elderly lady seated on a cushioned, gilt chair. She wore a red sari, lots of coloured bangles on her wrists, and golden earrings. Her hair was streaked with white, but her skin was still quite smooth and unlined, and she had large and very beautiful eyes.

'You must be Master Bond!' she said. 'Do you know who I am?'

'You're a lady with a birthday,' I said, 'but that's all I know. Dukhi didn't tell me anymore.'

'If you promise to keep it a secret, I'll tell you who I am. You see, everyone thinks I am mad. Do you think so, too?'

'I don't know.'

'Well, you must tell me if you think so,' she said with a chuckle. Her laugh was the sort of sound made by the gecko, coming from deep in the throat. 'I have a feeling you are a truthful boy. Do you find it very difficult to tell the truth?'

'Sometimes.'

'Sometimes. Of course, there are times when I tell lies—lots of little lies—because they're such fun! But would you call me a liar? I wouldn't, if I were you, but *would* you?'

'Are you a liar?'

'I'm asking you! If I were to tell you that I was a queen— that I am a queen—would you believe me?'

I thought deeply about this, and then said, 'I'll try to believe you.'

'Oh, but you *must* believe me. I am a real queen, I'm a rani. Look I've got diamonds to prove it.' And she held out her hands, and there was a ring on each finger, the stones glowing and glittering in the dim light. 'Diamonds, rubies, pearls and emeralds! Only a queen can have these!' She was most anxious that I should believe her.

'You must be a queen,' I said.

'Right!' she snapped. 'In that case, would you mind calling me "Your Highness"?'

'Your Highness,' I said.

She smiled. It was a slow, beautiful smile. All her face lit up.

'I could love you,' she said. 'But better still, I'll give you something to eat. Do you like chocolates?'

'Yes, Your Highness.'

'Well,' she said, taking a box from the table beside her, 'these have come all the way from England. Take two. Only two, mind you, otherwise the box will finish before Saturday, and I don't want that to happen because I won't get any more till Saturday. That's when Captain MacWhirr's ship sets in, the SS *Lucy* loaded with boxes and boxes of chocolates!'

'All for you?' I asked in considerable awe.

'Yes, of course. They have to last at least three months. I get them from England. I get only the best chocolates. I like them with pink, crunchy fillings, don't you?'

'Oh, yes!' I exclaimed, full of envy.

'Never mind,' she said. 'I may give you one now and then—if you're very nice to me. Here you are, help yourself...' She pushed the chocolate box towards me.

I took a silver-wrapped chocolate, and then just as I was thinking of taking a second one, she quickly took the box away.

'No more!' she said, 'They have to last till Saturday.'

'But I took only one,' I said with some indignation.

'Did you?' She gave me a sharp look, decided I was telling the truth, and said graciously, 'Well, in that case you can have another.'

Watching the rani carefully, in case she snatched the box away again, I selected a second chocolate, this one with a green wrapper. I don't remember what kind of a day it was outside, but I remember the bright green of the chocolate wrapper.

I thought it would be rude to eat the chocolates in front of a queen, so I put them in my pocket and said, 'I'd better go now. Ayah will be looking for me.'

'And when will you be coming to see me again?'

'I don't know,' I said.

'Your Highness.'

'Your Highness.'

'There's something I want you to do for me,' she said, placing one little finger on my shoulder and giving me a conspiratorial look. 'Will you do it?'

'What is it, Your Highness?'

'What is it? Why do you ask? A real prince never asks where or why or whatever, he simply does what the princess asks of him. When I was a princess—before I became a queen, that is—I asked a prince to swim across the lake and fetch me a lily growing on the other bank.'

'And did he get it for you?'

'He drowned halfway across. Let that be a lesson to you. Never agree to do something without knowing what it is.'

'But I thought you said...'

'Never mind what I *said*. It's what I *say* that matters!'

'Oh, all right,' I said, fidgeting to be gone. 'What is it you want me to do?'

'Nothing.' Her tiny rosebud lips pouted and she stared sullenly at a picture on the wall. Now that my eyes had grown used to the dim light in the room, I noticed that the walls were filled with portraits of stout rajas and ranis, turbaned and bedecked in fine clothes. There were also portraits of Queen Victoria and King George V of England. And, in the centre of all this distinguished company, a large picture of Mickey Mouse.

'I'll do it if it isn't too dangerous,' I said.

'Then listen.' She took my hand and drew me towards her— what a tiny hand she had!—and whispered, 'I want a red rose. From the palace garden. But be careful! Don't let Dukhi the gardener catch you. He'll know it's for me. He knows I love roses. And he hates me! I'll tell you why, one day. But if he catches you, he'll do something terrible.'

'To me?'

'No, to himself. That's much worse, isn't it? He'll tie himself into knots, or lie naked on a bed of thorns, or go on a long fast with nothing to eat but fruit, sweets and chicken! So you will be careful, won't you?'

'Oh, but he doesn't hate you,' I cried in protest, remembering the flowers he'd sent for her, and looking around, I found that I'd been sitting on them. 'Look, he sent these flowers for your birthday!'

'Well, if he sent them for my birthday, you can take them back,' she snapped. 'But if he sent them for me...' and she suddenly softened and looked coy, 'then I might keep them. Thank you, my dear, it was a very sweet thought.' And she leant forwards as though to kiss me.

'It's late, I must go!' I said in alarm, and turning on my heels, ran out of the room and down the spiral staircase.

A LONG WALK FOR BINA

I

A leopard, lithe and sinewy, drank at the mountain stream, and then lay down on the grass to bask in the late February sunshine. Its tail twitched occasionally and the animal appeared to be sleeping. At the sound of distant voices it raised its head to listen, then stood up and leapt lightly over the boulders in the stream, disappearing among the trees on the opposite bank.

A minute or two later, three children came walking down the forest path. They were a girl and two boys, and they were singing in their local dialect an old song they had learnt from their grandparents.

Five more miles to go!
We climb through rain and snow.
A river to cross...
A mountain to pass...
Now we've four more miles to go!

Their school satchels looked new, their clothes had been washed and pressed. Their loud and cheerful singing startled a spotted forktail. The bird left its favourite rock in the stream and flew down the dark ravine.

'Well, we have only three more miles to go,' said the bigger boy, Prakash, who had been this way hundreds of times. 'But first we have to cross the stream.'

He was a sturdy twelve-year-old with eyes like black currants and a mop of bushy hair that refused to settle down on his head. The girl and her small brother were taking this path for the first time.

'I'm feeling tired, Bina,' said the little boy.

Bina smiled at him, and Prakash said, 'Don't worry, Sonu, you'll get used to the walk. There's plenty of time.' He glanced at the old watch he'd been given by his grandfather. It needed constant winding. 'We can rest here for five or six minutes.'

They sat down on a smooth boulder and watched the clear water of the shallow stream tumbling downhill. Bina examined the old watch on Prakash's wrist. The glass was badly scratched and she could barely make out the figures on the dial. 'Are you sure it still gives the right time?' she asked.

'Well, it loses five minutes every day, so I put it ten minutes ahead at night. That means by morning it's quite accurate! Even our teacher, Mr Mani, asks me for the time. If he doesn't ask, I tell him! The clock in our classroom keeps stopping.'

They removed their shoes and let the cold mountain water run over their feet. Bina was the same age as Prakash. She had pink cheeks, soft brown eyes, and hair that was just beginning to lose its natural curls. Hers was a gentle face, but a determined little chin showed that she could be a strong person. Sonu, her younger brother, was ten. He was a thin boy who had been sickly as a child but was now beginning to fill out. Although he did not look very athletic, he could run like the wind.

Bina had been going to school in her own village of Koli, on the other side of the mountain. But it had been a primary school, finishing at Class 5. Now, in order to study in Class 6, she would have to walk several miles every day to Nauti, where there was a high school going up to Class 8. It had been decided that Sonu would also shift to the new school, to give Bina company. Prakash, their neighbour in Koli, was already a pupil at the Nauti school. His mischievous nature, which sometimes got him into trouble, had resulted in his having to repeat a year.

But this didn't seem to bother him. 'What's the hurry?' he had told his indignant parents. 'You're not sending me to a foreign land when I finish school. And our cows aren't running away, are they?'

'You would prefer to look after the cows, wouldn't you?' asked Bina, as they got up to continue their walk.

'Oh, school's all right. Wait till you see old Mr Mani. He always gets our names mixed up, as well as the subjects he's supposed to be teaching. At our last lesson, instead of maths, he gave us a geography lesson!'

'More fun than maths,' said Bina.

'Yes, but there's a new teacher this year. She's very young they say, just out of college. I wonder what she'll be like.'

Bina walked faster and Sonu had some trouble keeping up with them. She was excited about the new school and the prospect of different surroundings. She had seldom been outside her own village, with its small school and single ration shop. The day's routine never varied—helping her mother in the fields or with household tasks like fetching water from the spring or cutting grass and fodder for the cattle. Her father, who was a soldier, was away for nine months in the year and Sonu was still too small for the heavier tasks.

As they neared Nauti Village, they were joined by other children coming from different directions. Even where there were no major roads, the mountains were full of little lanes and shortcuts. Like a game of snakes and ladders, these narrow paths zigzagged around the hills and villages, cutting through fields and crossing narrow ravines until they came together to form a fairly busy road along which mules, cattle and goats joined the throng.

Nauti was a fairly large village, and from here a broader but dustier road started for Tehri. There was a small bus, several trucks and (for part of the way) a road roller. The road hadn't been completed because the heavy diesel roller couldn't take the steep climb to Nauti. It stood on the roadside halfway up the road from Tehri.

Prakash knew almost everyone in the area, and exchanged greetings and gossip with other children as well as with muleteers, bus drivers, milkmen and labourers working on the road. He loved telling everyone the time, even if they weren't interested.

'It's nine o'clock,' he would announce, glancing at his wrist. 'Isn't your bus leaving today?'

'Off with you!' the bus driver would respond, 'I'll leave when I'm ready.'

As the children approached Nauti, the small flat school buildings came into view on the outskirts of the village, fringed by a line of long-leaved pines. A small crowd had assembled on the one playing field. Something unusual seemed to have happened. Prakash ran forward to see what it was all about. Bina and Sonu stood aside, waiting in a patch of sunlight near the boundary wall.

Prakash soon came running back to them. He was bubbling over with excitement.

'It's Mr Mani!' he gasped. 'He's disappeared! People are saying a leopard must have carried him off!'

II

Mr Mani wasn't really old. He was about fifty-five and was expected to retire soon. But for the children, most adults over forty seemed ancient! And Mr Mani had always been a bit absent-minded, even as a young man.

He had gone out for his early morning walk, saying he'd be back by eight o'clock, in time to have his breakfast and be ready for class. He wasn't married, but his sister and her husband stayed with him. When it was past nine o'clock his sister presumed he'd stopped at a neighbour's house for breakfast (he loved tucking into other people's breakfast) and that he had gone on to school from there. But when the school bell rang at ten o'clock, and everyone but Mr Mani was present, questions were asked and guesses were made.

No one had seen him return from his walk and enquiries made in the village showed that he had not stopped at anyone's house. For Mr Mani to disappear was puzzling; for him to disappear without his breakfast was extraordinary.

Then a milkman returning from the next village said he had seen a leopard sitting on a rock on the outskirts of the pine forest. There had been talk of a cattle-killer in the valley, of leopards and other animals being displaced by the construction of a dam. But as yet no one had heard of a leopard attacking a man. Could Mr Mani have been its first victim? Someone found a strip of red cloth entangled in a blackberry bush and went running through the village showing it to everyone. Mr Mani had been known to wear red pyjamas. Surely he had been seized and eaten! But where were his remains? And why had he been in his pyjamas?

Meanwhile Bina and Sonu and the rest of the children had followed their teachers into the school playground. Feeling a little lost, Bina looked around for Prakash. She found herself facing a dark, slender young woman wearing spectacles, who must have been in her early twenties—just a little too old to be another student. She had a kind, expressive face and she seemed a little concerned by all that had been happening.

Bina noticed that she had lovely hands; it was obvious that the new teacher hadn't milked cows or worked in the fields!

'You must be new here,' said the teacher, smiling at Bina. 'And is this your little brother?'

'Yes, we've come from Koli Village. We were at school there.'

'It's a long walk from Koli. You didn't see any leopards, did you? Well, I'm new too. Are you in the sixth class?'

'Sonu is in the third. I'm in the sixth.'

'Then I'm your new teacher. My name is Tania Ramola. Come along, let's see if we can settle down in our classroom.'

Mr Mani turned up at twelve o'clock, wondering what all the fuss was about. No, he snapped, he had not been attacked by a leopard; and yes, he had lost his pyjamas and would someone kindly return them to him?

'How did you lose your pyjamas, sir?' asked Prakash.

'They were blown off the washing line!' snapped Mr Mani.

After much questioning, Mr Mani admitted that he had gone further than he had intended, and that he had lost his way coming back. He had been a bit upset because the new teacher, a slip of a girl, had been given charge of the sixth, while he was still with the fifth, along with that troublesome boy Prakash, who kept on reminding him of the time! The Headmaster had explained that as Mr Mani was due to retire at the end of the year, the school did not wish to burden him with a senior class. But Mr Mani looked upon the whole thing as a plot to get rid of him. He glowered at Miss Ramola whenever he passed her. And when she smiled back at him, he looked the other way!

Mr Mani had been getting even more absent-minded of late—putting on his shoes without his socks, wearing his homespun waistcoat inside out, mixing up people's names and, of course, eating other people's lunches and dinners. His sister had made a mutton broth for the postmaster, who was down with 'flu', and had asked Mr Mani to take it over in a thermos. When the postmaster opened the thermos, he found only a few drops of broth at the bottom—Mr Mani had drunk the rest somewhere along the way.

When sometimes Mr Mani spoke of his coming retirement, it was to describe his plans for the small field he owned just behind the house. Right now, it was full of potatoes, which did not require much looking after; but he had plans for growing dahlias, roses, French beans, and other fruits and flowers.

The next time he visited Tehri, he promised himself, he would buy some dahlia bulbs and rose cuttings. The monsoon season would be a good time to put them down. And meanwhile, his potatoes were still flourishing.

III

Bina enjoyed her first day at the new school. She felt at ease with Miss Ramola, as did most of the boys and girls in her class. Tania Ramola had been to distant towns such as Delhi and Lucknow—places they had only heard about—and it was said that she had a brother who was a pilot and flew planes all over the world. Perhaps he'd fly over Nauti some day!

Most of the children had of course seen planes flying overhead, but none of them had seen a ship, and only a few had been on a train. Tehri mountain was far from the railway and hundreds of miles from the sea. But they all knew about the big dam that was being built at Tehri, just forty miles away.

Bina, Sonu and Prakash had company for part of the way home, but gradually the other children went off in different directions. Once they had crossed the stream, they were on their own again.

It was a steep climb all the way back to their village. Prakash had a supply of peanuts which he shared with Bina and Sonu, and at a small spring they quenched their thirst.

When they were less than a mile from home, they met a postman who had finished his round of the villages in the area and was now returning to Nauti.

'Don't waste time along the way,' he told them. 'Try to get home before dark.'

'What's the hurry?' asked Prakash, glancing at his watch. 'It's only five o'clock.'

'There's a leopard around. I saw it this morning, not far from the stream. No one is sure how it got here. So don't take any chances. Get home early.'

'So, there really is a leopard,' said Sonu.

They took his advice and walked faster, and Sonu forgot to complain about his aching feet.

They were home well before sunset.

There was a smell of cooking in the air and they were hungry.

'Cabbage and roti,' said Prakash gloomily. 'But I could eat anything today.' He stopped outside his small slate-roofed house, and Bina and Sonu waved goodbye and carried on across a couple of ploughed fields until they reached their small stone house.

'Stuffed tomatoes,' said Sonu, sniffing just outside the front door.

'And lemon pickle,' said Bina, who had helped cut, sun and salt the lemons a month previously.

Their mother was lighting the kitchen stove. They greeted her with great hugs and demands for an immediate dinner. She was a good cook who could make even the simplest of dishes taste delicious. Her favourite saying was, 'Home-made bread is better than roast meat abroad,' and Bina and Sonu had to agree.

Electricity had yet to reach their village, and they took their meal by the light of a kerosene lamp. After the meal, Sonu settled down to do a little homework, while Bina stepped outside to look at the stars.

Across the fields, someone was playing a flute. 'It must be Prakash,' thought Bina. 'He always breaks off on the high notes.' But the flute music was simple and appealing, and she began singing softly to herself in the dark.

IV

Mr Mani was having trouble with the porcupines. They had been getting into his garden at night and digging up and eating his potatoes. From his bedroom window—left open now that the mild April weather had arrived—he could listen to them enjoying the vegetables he had worked hard to grow. Scrunch, scrunch! katar, katar, as their sharp teeth sliced through the largest and juiciest of potatoes. For Mr Mani it was as though they were biting through his own flesh. And the sound of them digging industriously as they rooted up those healthy, leafy plants made him tremble with rage and indignation. The unfairness of it all!

Yes, Mr Mani hated porcupines. He prayed for their destruction, their removal from the face of the earth. But, as his friends were quick to point out, 'The creator made porcupines too,' and in any case you could never see the creatures or catch them, they were completely nocturnal.

Mr Mani got out of bed every night, torch in one hand, a stout stick in the other but, as soon as he stepped into the garden, the crunching and digging stopped and he was greeted by the most infuriating of silences. He would grope around in the dark, swinging wildly with the stick, but not a single porcupine was to be seen or heard. As soon as he was back in bed, the sounds would start all over again—scrunch, scrunch, katar, katar...

Mr Mani came to his class tired and dishevelled, with rings under his eyes and a permanent frown on his face. It took some time for his pupils to discover the reason for his misery, but when they did, they felt sorry for their teacher and took to discussing ways and means of saving his potatoes from the porcupines.

It was Prakash who came up with the idea of a moat or water ditch. 'Porcupines don't like water,' he said knowledgeably.

'How do you know?' asked one of his friends.

'Throw water on one and see how it runs! They don't like getting their quills wet.'

There was no one who could disprove Prakash's theory, and the class fell in with the idea of building a moat, especially as it meant getting most of the day off.

'Anything to make Mr Mani happy,' said the Headmaster, and the rest of the school watched with envy as the pupils of Class 5, armed with spades and shovels collected from all parts of the village, took up their positions around Mr Mani's potato field and began digging a ditch.

By evening the moat was ready, but it was still dry and the

porcupines got in again that night and had a great feast.

'At this rate,' said Mr Mani gloomily, 'there won't be any potatoes left to save.'

But the next day, Prakash and the other boys and girls managed to divert the water from a stream that flowed past the village. They had the satisfaction of watching it flow gently into the ditch. Everyone went home in a good mood. By nightfall, the ditch had overflowed, the potato field was flooded, and Mr Mani found himself trapped inside his house. But Prakash and his friends had won the day. The porcupines stayed away that night!

⁊

A month had passed, and wild violets, daisies and buttercups now sprinkled the hill slopes and, on her way to school, Bina gathered enough to make a little posy. The bunch of flowers fitted easily into an old ink well. Miss Ramola was delighted to find this little display in the middle of her desk.

'Who put these here?' she asked in surprise.

Bina kept quiet, and the rest of the class smiled secretively. After that, they took turns bringing flowers for the classroom.

On her long walks to school and home again, Bina became aware that April was the month of new leaves. The oak leaves were bright green above and silver beneath, and when they rippled in the breeze they were clouds of silvery green. The path was strewn with old leaves, dry and crackly. Sonu loved kicking them around.

Clouds of white butterflies floated across the stream. Sonu was chasing a butterfly when he stumbled over something dark and repulsive. He went sprawling on the grass. When he got to his feet, he looked down at the remains of a small animal.

'Bina! Prakash! Come quickly!' he shouted.

It was part of a sheep, killed some days earlier by a much larger animal.

'Only a leopard could have done this,' said Prakash.

'Let's get away, then,' said Sonu. 'It might still be around!'

'No, there's nothing left to eat. The leopard will be hunting elsewhere by now. Perhaps it's moved on to the next valley.'

'Still, I'm frightened,' said Sonu. 'There may be more leopards!'

Bina took him by the hand. 'Leopards don't attack humans!' she said.

'They will, if they get a taste for people!' insisted Prakash.

'Well, this one hasn't attacked any people as yet,' said Bina, although she couldn't be sure. Hadn't there been rumours of a leopard attacking some workers near the dam? But she did not want Sonu to feel afraid, so she did not mention the story. All she said was, 'It has probably come here because of all the activity near the dam.'

All the same, they hurried home. And for a few days, whenever they reached the stream, they crossed over very quickly, unwilling to linger too long at that lovely spot.

V

A few days later, a school party was on its way to Tehri to see the new dam that was being built.

Miss Ramola had arranged to take her class, and Mr Mani, not wishing to be left out, insisted on taking his class as well. That meant there were about fifty boys and girls taking part in the outing. The little bus could only take thirty. A friendly truck driver agreed to take some children if they were prepared to sit on sacks of potatoes. And Prakash persuaded the owner of the diesel roller to turn it around and head it back to Tehri—with him and a couple of friends up on the driving seat.

Prakash's small group set off at sunrise, as they had to walk some distance in order to reach the stranded road roller. The bus left at 9 a.m. with Miss Ramola and her class, and Mr Mani and some of his pupils. The truck was to follow later.

It was Bina's first visit to a large town, and her first bus ride.

The sharp curves along the winding, downhill road made several children feel sick. The bus driver seemed to be in a tearing hurry. He took them along at a rolling, rollicking speed, which made Bina feel quite giddy. She rested her head on her arms and refused to look out of the window. Hairpin bends and cliff edges, pine forests and snow-capped peaks, all swept past her, but she felt too ill to want to look at anything. It was just as well—those sudden drops, hundreds of feet to the valley below, were quite frightening. Bina began to wish that she hadn't come—or that she had joined Prakash on the road roller instead!

Miss Ramola and Mr Mani didn't seem to notice the lurching and groaning of the old bus. They had made this journey many times. They were busy arguing about the advantages and disadvantages of large dams—an argument that was to continue on and off for much of the day.

Meanwhile, Prakash and his friends had reached the roller. The driver hadn't turned up, but they managed to reverse it and get it going in the direction of Tehri. They were soon overtaken by both bus and truck but kept moving along at a steady chug. Prakash spotted Bina at the window of the bus and waved cheerfully. She responded feebly.

Bina felt better when the road levelled out near Tehri. As they crossed an old bridge over the wide river, they were startled by a loud bang which made the bus shudder. A cloud of dust rose above the town.

'They're blasting the mountain,' said Miss Ramola.

'End of a mountain,' said Mr Mani, mournfully.

While they were drinking cups of tea at the bus stop, waiting for the potato truck and the road roller, Miss Ramola and Mr Mani continued their argument about the dam. Miss Ramola maintained that it would bring electric power and water for irrigation to large areas of the country, including the surrounding area. Mr Mani declared that it was a menace, as it was situated in an earthquake zone. There would be a terrible disaster if the dam burst! Bina found it all very confusing. And what about the animals in the area, she wondered, what would happen to them?

The argument was becoming quite heated when the potato truck arrived. There was no sign of the road roller, so it was decided that Mr Mani should wait for Prakash and his friends while Miss Ramola's group went ahead.

⁓

Some eight or nine miles before Tehri, the road roller had broken down, and Prakash and his friends were forced to walk. They had not gone far, however, when a mule train came along—five or six mules that had been delivering sacks of grain in Nauti. A boy rode on the first mule, but the others had no loads.

'Can you give us a ride to Tehri?' called Prakash.

'Make yourselves comfortable,' said the boy.

There were no saddles, only gunny sacks strapped on to the mules with rope. They had a rough but jolly ride down to the Tehri bus stop. None of them had ever ridden mules; but they had saved at least an hour on the road.

Looking around the bus stop for the rest of the party, they could find no one from their school. And Mr Mani, who should have been waiting for them, had vanished.

VI

Tania Ramola and her group had taken the steep road to the hill above Tehri. Half an hour's climbing brought them to a little plateau which overlooked the town, the river and the dam site.

The earthworks for the dam were only just coming up, but a wide tunnel had been bored through the mountain to divert the river into another channel. Down below, the old town was still spread out across the valley and from a distance it looked quite charming and picturesque.

'Will the whole town be swallowed up by the waters of the dam?' asked Bina.

'Yes, all of it,' said Miss Ramola. 'The clock tower and the old palace. The long bazaar, and the temples, the schools and the jail, and hundreds of houses, for many miles up the valley. All those people will have to go—thousands of them! Of course they'll be resettled elsewhere.'

'But the town's been here for hundreds of years,' said Bina. 'They were quite happy without the dam, weren't they?'

'I suppose they were. But the dam isn't just for them—it's for the millions who live further downstream, across the plains.'

'And it doesn't matter what happens to this place?'

'The local people will be given new homes somewhere else.' Miss Ramola found herself on the defensive and decided to change the subject. 'Everyone must be hungry. It's time we had our lunch.'

Bina kept quiet. She didn't think the local people would want to go away. And it was a good thing, she mused, that there was only a small stream and not a big river running past her village. To be uprooted like this—a town and hundreds of villages—and put down somewhere on the hot, dusty plains—seemed to her unbearable.

'Well, I'm glad I don't live in Tehri,' she said.

She did not know it, but all the animals and most of the birds had already left the area. The leopard had been among them.

⁓

They walked through the colourful, crowded bazaar, where fruit sellers did business beside silversmiths, and pavement vendors sold everything from umbrellas to glass bangles. Sparrows attacked sacks of grain, monkeys made off with bananas, and stray cows and dogs rummaged in refuse bins, but nobody took any notice. Music blared from radios. Buses blew their horns. Sonu bought a whistle to add to the general din, but Miss Ramola told him to put it away. Bina had kept five rupees aside, and now she used it to buy a cotton headscarf for her mother.

As they were about to enter a small restaurant for a meal, they were joined by Prakash and his companions; but of Mr

Mani there was still no sign.

'He must have met one of his relatives,' said Prakash. 'He has relatives everywhere.'

After a simple meal of rice and lentils, they walked the length of the bazaar without finding Mr Mani. At last, when they were about to give up the search, they saw him emerge from a by-lane, a large sack slung over his shoulder.

'Sir, where have you been?' asked Prakash. 'We have been looking for you everywhere.'

On Mr Mani's face was a look of triumph.

'Help me with this bag,' he said breathlessly.

'You've bought more potatoes, sir,' said Prakash.

'Not potatoes, boy. Dahlia bulbs!'

VII

It was dark by the time they were all back in Nauti. Mr Mani had refused to be separated from his sack of dahlia bulbs, and had been forced to sit in the back of the truck with Prakash and most of the boys.

Bina did not feel so ill on the return journey. Going uphill was definitely better than going downhill! But by the time the bus reached Nauti it was too late for most of the children to walk back to the more distant villages. The boys were put up in different homes, while the girls were given beds in the school veranda.

The night was warm and still. Large moths fluttered around the single bulb that lit the veranda. Counting moths, Sonu soon fell asleep. But Bina stayed awake for some time, listening to the sounds of the night. A nightjar went tonk-tonk in the bushes, and somewhere in the forest an owl hooted softly. The sharp call of a barking deer travelled up the valley from the direction of the stream. Jackals kept howling. It seemed that there were more of them than ever before.

Bina was not the only one to hear the barking deer. The

leopard, stretched full length on a rocky ledge, heard it too. The leopard raised its head and then got up slowly. The deer was its natural prey. But there weren't many left, and that was why the leopard, robbed of its forest by the dam, had taken to attacking dogs and cattle near the villages.

As the cry of the barking deer sounded nearer, the leopard left its lookout point and moved swiftly through the shadows towards the stream.

VIII

In early June the hills were dry and dusty, and forest fires broke out, destroying shrubs and trees, killing birds and small animals. The resin in the pines made these trees burn more fiercely, and the wind would take sparks from the trees and carry them into the dry grass and leaves, so that new fires would spring up before the old ones had died out. Fortunately, Bina's village was not in the pine belt; the fires did not reach it. But Nauti was surrounded by a fire that raged for three days, and the children had to stay away from school.

And then, towards the end of June, the monsoon rains arrived and there was an end to forest fires. The monsoon lasts three months and the lower Himalayas would be drenched in rain, mist and cloud for the next three months.

The first rain arrived while Bina, Prakash and Sonu were returning home from school. Those first few drops on the dusty path made them cry out with excitement. Then the rain grew heavier and a wonderful aroma rose from the earth.

'The best smell in the world!' exclaimed Bina.

Everything suddenly came to life. The grass, the crops, the trees, the birds. Even the leaves of the trees glistened and looked new.

That first wet weekend, Bina and Sonu helped their mother plant beans, maize and cucumbers. Sometimes, when the rain was very heavy, they had to run indoors. Otherwise they worked in the rain, the soft mud clinging to their bare legs.

Prakash now owned a dog, a black dog with one ear up and one ear down. The dog ran around getting in everyone's way, barking at cows, goats, hens and humans, without frightening any of them. Prakash said it was a very clever dog, but no one else seemed to think so. Prakash also said it would protect the village from the leopard, but others said the dog would be the first to be taken—he'd run straight into the jaws of Mr Spots!

In Nauti, Tania Ramola was trying to find a dry spot in the quarters she'd been given. It was an old building and the roof was leaking in several places. Mugs and buckets were scattered about the floor in order to catch the drips.

Mr Mani had dug up all his potatoes and presented them to the friends and neighbours who had given him lunches and dinners. He was having the time of his life, planting dahlia bulbs all over his garden.

'I'll have a field of many-coloured dahlias!' he announced. 'Just wait till the end of August!'

'Watch out for those porcupines,' warned his sister. 'They eat dahlia bulbs too!'

Mr Mani made an inspection tour of his moat, no longer in flood, and found everything in good order. Prakash had done his job well.

☙

Now, when the children crossed the stream, they found that the water level had risen by about a foot. Small cascades had turned into waterfalls. Ferns had sprung up on the banks. Frogs chanted.

Prakash and his dog dashed across the stream. Bina and Sonu followed more cautiously. The current was much stronger now and the water was almost up to their knees. Once they had crossed the stream, they hurried along the path, anxious not to be caught in a sudden downpour.

By the time they reached school, each of them had two

or three leeches clinging to their legs. They had to use salt to remove them. The leeches were the most troublesome part of the rainy season. Even the leopard did not like them. It could not lie in the long grass without getting leeches on its paws and face.

One day, when Bina, Prakash and Sonu were about to cross the stream they heard a low rumble, which grew louder every second. Looking up at the opposite hill, they saw several trees shudder, tilt outwards and begin to fall. Earth and rocks bulged out from the mountain, then came crashing down into the ravine.

'Landslide!' shouted Sonu.

'It's carried away the path,' said Bina. 'Don't go any further.'

There was a tremendous roar as more rocks, trees and bushes fell away and crashed down the hillside.

Prakash's dog, who had gone ahead, came running back, tail between his legs.

They remained rooted to the spot until the rocks had stopped falling and the dust had settled. Birds circled the area, calling wildly. A frightened barking deer ran past them.

'We can't go to school now,' said Prakash. 'There's no way around.'

They turned and trudged home through the gathering mist.

In Koli, Prakash's parents had heard the roar of the landslide. They were setting out in search of the children when they saw them emerge from the mist, waving cheerfully.

IX

They had to miss school for another three days, and Bina was afraid they might not be able to take their final exams. Although Prakash was not really troubled at the thought of missing exams, he did not like feeling helpless just because their path had been swept away. So he explored the hillside until he found a goat-track going around the mountain. It joined up with another path near

Nauti. This made their walk longer by a mile, but Bina did not mind. It was much cooler now that the rains were in full swing.

The only trouble with the new route was that it passed close to the leopard's lair. The animal had made this area its own since being forced to leave the dam area.

One day Prakash's dog ran ahead of them barking furiously. Then he ran back whimpering.

'He's always running away from something,' observed Sonu. But a minute later he understood the reason for the dog's fear.

They rounded a bend and Sonu saw the leopard standing in their way. They were struck dumb—too terrified to run. It was a strong, sinewy creature. A low growl rose from its throat. It seemed ready to spring.

They stood perfectly still, afraid to move or say a word. And the leopard must have been equally surprised. It stared at them for a few seconds, then bounded across the path and into the oak forest.

Sonu was shaking. Bina could hear her heart hammering. Prakash could only stammer: 'Did you see the way he sprang? Wasn't he beautiful?'

He forgot to look at his watch for the rest of the day.

A few days later, Sonu stopped and pointed to a large outcrop of rock on the next hill.

The leopard stood far above them, outlined against the sky. It looked strong, majestic. Standing beside it were two young cubs.

'Look at those little ones!' exclaimed Sonu.

'So it's a female, not a male,' said Prakash.

'That's why she was killing so often,' said Bina. 'She had to feed her cubs too.'

They remained still for several minutes, gazing up at the leopard and her cubs. The leopard family took no notice of them.

'She knows we are here,' said Prakash, 'but she doesn't care. She knows we won't harm them.'

'We are cubs too!' said Sonu.

'Yes,' said Bina. 'And there's still plenty of space for all of us. Even when the dam is ready there will still be room for leopards and humans.'

X

The school exams were over. The rains were nearly over too. The landslide had been cleared, and Bina, Prakash and Sonu were once again crossing the stream.

There was a chill in the air, for it was the end of September.

Prakash had learnt to play the flute quite well, and he played on the way to school and then again on the way home. As a result he did not look at his watch so often. One morning they found a small crowd in front of Mr Mani's house.

'What could have happened?' wondered Bina. 'I hope he hasn't got lost again.'

'Maybe he's sick,' said Sonu.

'Maybe it's the porcupines,' said Prakash.

But it was none of these things.

Mr Mani's first dahlia was in bloom, and half the village had turned up to look at it! It was a huge red double dahlia, so heavy that it had to be supported with sticks. No one had ever seen such a magnificent flower!

Mr Mani was a happy man. And his mood only improved over the coming week, as more and more dahlias flowered—crimson, yellow, purple, mauve, white—button dahlias, pom-pom dahlias, spotted dahlias, striped dahlias... Mr Mani had them all! A dahlia even turned up on Tania Ramola's desk—he got along quite well with her now—and another brightened up the Headmaster's study.

A week later, on their way home—it was almost the last day of the school term—Bina, Prakash and Sonu talked about what they might do when they grew up.

'I think I'll become a teacher,' said Bina. 'I'll teach children about animals and birds, and trees and flowers.'

'Better than maths!' said Prakash.

'I'll be a pilot,' said Sonu. 'I want to fly a plane like Miss Ramola's brother.'

'And what about you, Prakash?' asked Bina.

Prakash just smiled and said, 'Maybe I'll be a flute player,' and he put the flute to his lips and played a sweet melody.

'Well, the world needs flute players too,' said Bina, as they fell into step beside him.

The leopard had been stalking a barking deer. She paused when she heard the flute and the voices of the children. Her own young ones were growing quickly, but the girl and the two boys did not look much older.

They had started singing their favourite song again.

Five more miles to go!
We climb through rain and snow,
A river to cross...
A mountain to pass...
Now we've four more miles to go!

The leopard waited until they had passed, before returning to the trail of the barking deer.

WHEN GUAVAS ARE RIPE

Guava trees are easy to climb. And guavas are good to eat. So it's little wonder that an orchard of guava trees is a popular place with boys and girls.

Just across the road from Ranji's house, on the other side of a low wall, was a large guava orchard. The monsoon rains were almost over. It was a warm humid day in September, and the guavas were ripening, turning from green to gold—no longer hard, but growing soft and sweet and juicy.

The schools were closed because of a religious festival. Ranji's father was at work. Ranji's mother was enjoying an afternoon siesta on a cot in the backyard. His grandmother was busy teaching her pet parrot to recite a prayer.

'I feel like getting into those guava trees,' said Ranji to himself. 'It's months since I climbed a tree.'

He was soon across the road and over the wall and into the trees. He chose a tree that grew in the middle of the orchard, where it was unlikely that he would be disturbed, then he climbed swiftly into its branches. A cluster of guavas swung just above him. He reached up for one of them, but to his surprise he found himself clutching a small bare foot which had suddenly been thrust through the foliage.

Having caught the foot, Ranji did not let go. Instead he pulled hard on it. There was a squeal and someone came toppling down on him. Ranji found himself clutching at arms and legs. Together they crashed through a couple of branches and landed with a thud on the soft ground beneath the tree.

Ranji and the intruder struggled fiercely. They rolled about on the grass. Ranji tried a judo hold—without any success. Then he saw that his opponent was a girl. It was his friend and neighbour, Koki.

'It's you!' he gasped.

'It's me,' said Koki. 'And what are *you* doing here?'

'Get your knee out of my stomach and I'll tell you.'

When he recovered his breath, he said, 'I just felt like climbing a tree.'

'So did I.'

He stared at her. There was guava juice at the corners of her mouth and on her chin.

'Are the guavas good?' he asked.

'Quite sweet, in this tree,' said Koki. 'You find another tree for yourself, Ranji. There must be thirty or forty trees to choose from.'

'And all going to waste,' said Ranji. 'Look, some of the guavas have been spoilt by the birds.'

'Nobody wants them, it seems.'

Koki climbed back into her tree, and Ranji obligingly walked a little further and climbed another tree. After a few polite exchanges they fell silent, their attention given over entirely to the eating of guavas.

'I've eaten five,' said Koki after some time.

'You'd better stop.'

'You're only saying that because you've just started.'

'Well, three's enough for me.'

'I'm getting a tummy ache, I think.'

'I warned you. Come on, I'll take you home. We can come back tomorrow. There are still lots of guavas left. Hundreds!'

'I don't think I want to eat any more,' said Koki.

She felt better the next day—so well, in fact, that Ranji found her leaning on the gate, waiting for him to join her. She was accompanied by her small brother, Teju, who was only six and very mischievous.

'How are you feeling today?' asked Ranji.

'Hungry,' said Koki.

'Why did you bring your brother?'

'He wants to start climbing trees.'

Soon they were in the orchard. Ranji and Koki helped Teju into the branches of one of the smaller trees and then made for other trees, disturbing a party of parrots who flew in circles around the orchard, screaming their protests.

Two boys and a girl talking to each other from three different trees can make quite a lot of noise, and it wasn't only the birds who were disturbed. Though they did not know it, the orchard belonged to a wealthy property dealer and he employed a watchman, whose duty was to keep away birds, children, monkeys, flying foxes and other fruit-eating pests. But on a hot, sultry afternoon Gopal, the watchman, could not resist taking a nap. He was stretched out under a shady jackfruit tree, snoring so loudly that the flies that had been buzzing around him felt that a storm was brewing and kept their distance.

He woke to the sound of voices raised high in glee. Sitting up, he brushed a ladybird from his long moustache, then seized his lathi.

'Who's there?' he shouted, struggling to his feet.

There was a sudden silence in the trees.

'Who's there?' he called again.

No answer.

'I must have been dreaming,' he muttered, and was preparing to lie down and take another nap when Teju, who had been watching him, burst into laughter.

'Ho!' shouted the watchman, coming to life again.

'Thieves! I'll settle you!' And he began striding towards the centre of the orchard, boasting all the time of his physical prowess.

'I am not afraid of thieves, bandits, or wild beasts! I'll have you know that I was once the wrestling champion of an entire district of Dehra. Come on out and fight me if you dare!'

'Run!' hissed Koki, scrambling down her tree.

'Run!' shouted Ranji, as though it were a cricket match.

Teju was so startled by the sudden activity that he tumbled out of his tree and began crying, and Ranji and Koki had to go to his aid.

The sight of an enormous ex-wrestler bearing down on them was enough to make Teju stop crying and get to his feet. Then all three were fleeing across the grove, the watchman a little way behind them, waving his lathi and shouting at the top of his voice. Although he was an ex-wrestler (or perhaps because of it) he could not run very fast, and was still huffing and puffing some twenty metres behind them when they climbed up and over the wall. He could not climb walls either.

They ran off in different directions before returning home.

⁂

The next day, Ranji met Koki and Teju at the far end of the road.

'Is he there?' asked Koki.

'I haven't seen him. But he must be around somewhere.'

'Maybe he's gone for his lunch. We'll just walk past and take a quick look.'

The three of them strolled casually down the road. Koki said the gardens were looking very pretty. Teju gazed admiringly at a boy flying a kite from a rooftop. Ranji kept one eye on the road and one eye on the orchard wall. A squirrel ran along the top of the wall; the parrots were back in the guava trees.

They moved closer to the wall. Ranji leaned casually against it and Koki began to pick little daisies growing at the edge of the road. Teju, unable to hide his curiosity, pulled himself up on the wall and looked over. At the same time Gopal, the watchman, who had been hiding behind the wall waiting for them, stood up slowly and glared fiercely at Teju.

Teju gulped, but he did not flinch. He was looking straight into the watchman's red angry eyes.

'And what can I do for you?' said Gopal.

'I was just looking,' said Teju.

'At what?'

'At the view.'

Gopal was a little baffled. They looked just like the children he'd chased away yesterday, but he couldn't be sure. They didn't *look* guilty. But did children ever look guilty?

'There's a better view from the other side of the road,' he said gruffly. 'Now be off!'

'What lovely guavas,' said Koki, smiling sweetly. There weren't many people who could resist that smile!

'True,' said Ranji, with the air of one who was an expert on guavas and all things good to eat. 'They are just the right size and colour. I don't think I've seen better. But they'll be spoilt by the birds if you don't gather them soon.'

'It's none of your business,' said the watchman.

'Just look at his muscles,' said Teju, trying a different approach. 'He's really strong!'

Gopal looked pleased for once. He was proud of his former prowess, even though he was now rather flabby around the waist.

'You look like a wrestler,' said Ranji.

'I *am* a wrestler,' said Gopal.

'I told you so,' said Koki. 'What else could he be?'

'I'm a retired wrestler,' said Gopal.

'You don't look retired,' said Teju, fast learning that flattery can get you almost anywhere.

Gopal swelled with pride; such admiration hadn't come his way for a long time. To Koki he looked like a bullfrog swelling up, but she thought it better not to say so.

'Do you want to see my muscles?' he asked.

'Yes, yes!' they cried. 'Do show us!'

Gopal peeled off his shirt and thumped his chest. It sounded like a drum. They were really impressed. Then he bent his elbow and his biceps stood up like cricket balls.

'You can touch them,' he said generously.

Teju poked a finger into Gopal's biceps.

'Mister Universe!' he exclaimed.

Gopal glowed all over. He liked these children. How intelligent they were! Not everyone had the sense to appreciate his strength, his manliness, his magnificent physique!

'Climb over the wall and join me,' he said. 'Come sit on the grass and I'll tell you about the time when I was a wrestling champion.'

Over the wall they came, and sat politely on the grass. Gopal told them about some of his exploits, how he had vanquished a world-famous wrestler in five seconds flat, and how he had saved a carload of travellers from drowning by single-handedly dragging their car out of a river. They listened patiently. Then Teju mentioned that he was feeling hungry.

'Hungry?' said Gopal. 'Why didn't you tell me before? I'll bring you some guavas, that's all there is to eat here. I know which tree has the best ones. And they're all going to rot if no one eats them—no one's buying the crop this year, the owner's price is too high!'

Gopal hurried off and soon returned with a basket full of guavas.

'Help yourselves,' he said. 'But don't eat too many, you'll get sick.'

So they munched guavas and listened to Gopal tell them about the time he was waylaid by three bandits and how he threw them all into the village pond.

'Will you come again tomorrow?' asked Gopal eagerly, when the guavas were finished and the children got up to leave. 'Come tomorrow and I'll tell you another story.'

'We'll come tomorrow,' said Teju, looking at all the guava

trees laden with fruit.

Somehow it seemed very important to Gopal that they should come again. It was lonely in the orchard. Koki sensed this, and said, 'We like your stories.'

'They are good stories,' said Ranji, even if they were not entirely true, he thought...

They climbed over the wall and waved goodbye to Gopal.

◦

They came again the next day.

And even when the guava season was over and Gopal had nothing to offer them but his stories, they went to see him because by that time they had grown to like him.

THE NIGHT TRAIN AT DEOLI

When I was at college I used to spend my summer vacations in Dehra, at my grandmother's place. I would leave the plains early in May and return late in July. Deoli was a small station about thirty miles from Dehra. It marked the beginning of the heavy jungles of the Indian terai.

The train would reach Deoli at about five in the morning when the station would be dimly lit with electric bulbs and oil lamps, and the jungle across the railway tracks would just be visible in the faint light of dawn. Deoli had only one platform, an office for the stationmaster and a waiting room. The platform boasted a tea stall, a fruit vendor and a few stray dogs; not much else because the train stopped there for only ten minutes before rushing on into the forests.

Why it stopped at Deoli, I don't know. Nothing ever happened there. Nobody got off the train and nobody got on. There were never any coolies on the platform. But the train would halt there a full ten minutes and then a bell would sound, the guard would blow his whistle, and presently Deoli would be left behind and forgotten.

I used to wonder what happened in Deoli behind the station walls. I always felt sorry for that lonely little platform and for the place that nobody wanted to visit. I decided that one day I would get off the train at Deoli and spend the day there just to please the town.

I was eighteen, visiting my grandmother, and the night train stopped at Deoli. A girl came down the platform selling baskets.

It was a cold morning and the girl had a shawl thrown across her shoulders. Her feet were bare and her clothes were old but she was a young girl, walking gracefully and with dignity.

When she came to my window, she stopped. She saw that I was looking at her intently, but at first she pretended not to notice. She had pale skin, set off by shiny black hair and dark, troubled eyes. And then those eyes, searching and eloquent, met mine.

She stood by my window for some time and neither of us said anything. But when she moved on, I found myself leaving my seat and going to the carriage door. I stood waiting on the platform looking the other way. I walked across to the tea stall. A kettle was boiling over a small fire, but the owner of the stall was busy serving tea somewhere on the train. The girl followed me behind the stall.

'Do you want to buy a basket?' she asked. 'They are very strong, made of the finest cane...'

'No,' I said, 'I don't want a basket.'

We stood looking at each other for what seemed a very long time, and she said, 'Are you sure you don't want a basket?'

'All right, give me one,' I said, and took the one on top and gave her a rupee, hardly daring to touch her fingers.

As she was about to speak, the guard blew his whistle. She said something, but it was lost in the clanging of the bell and the hissing of the engine. I had to run back to my compartment. The carriage shuddered and jolted forward.

I watched her as the platform slipped away. She was alone on the platform and she did not move, but she was looking at me and smiling. I watched her until the signal box came in the way and then the jungle hid the station. But I could still see her standing there alone...

I stayed awake for the rest of the journey. I could not rid my mind of the picture of the girl's face and her dark, smouldering eyes.

But when I reached Dehra the incident became blurred and

distant, for there were other things to occupy my mind. It was only when I was making the return journey, two months later, that I remembered the girl.

I was looking out for her as the train drew into the station, and I felt an unexpected thrill when I saw her walking up the platform. I sprang off the footboard and waved to her.

When she saw me, she smiled. She was pleased that I remembered her. I was pleased that she remembered me. We were both pleased and it was almost like a meeting of old friends.

She did not go down the length of the train selling baskets but came straight to the tea stall. Her dark eyes were suddenly filled with light. We said nothing for some time but we couldn't have been more eloquent.

I felt the impulse to put her on the train there and then, and take her away with me. I could not bear the thought of having to watch her recede into the distance of Deoli station. I took the baskets from her hand and put them down on the ground. She put out her hand for one of them, but I caught her hand and held it.

'I have to go to Delhi,' I said.

She nodded. 'I do not have to go anywhere.'

The guard blew his whistle for the train to leave, and how I hated the guard for doing that.

'I will come again,' I said. 'Will you be here?'

She nodded again and, as she nodded, the bell clanged and the train slid forward. I had to wrench my hand away from the girl and run for the moving train.

This time I did not forget her. She was with me for the remainder of the journey and for long after. All that year she was a bright, living thing. And when the college term finished, I packed in haste and left for Dehra earlier than usual. My grandmother would be pleased at my eagerness to see her.

I was nervous and anxious as the train drew into Deoli, because I was wondering what I should say to the girl and what

I should do. I was determined that I wouldn't stand helplessly before her, hardly able to speak or do anything about my feelings.

The train came to Deoli, and I looked up and down the platform but I could not see the girl anywhere.

I opened the door and stepped off the footboard. I was deeply disappointed and overcome by a sense of foreboding. I felt I had to do something and so I ran up to the stationmaster and said, 'Do you know the girl who used to sell baskets here?'

'No, I don't,' said the stationmaster. 'And you'd better get on the train if you don't want to be left behind.'

But I paced up and down the platform and stared over the railings at the station yard. All I saw was a mango tree and a dusty road leading into the jungle. Where did the road go? The train was moving out of the station and I had to run up the platform and jump for the door of my compartment. Then, as the train gathered speed and rushed through the forests, I sat brooding in front of the window.

What could I do about finding a girl I had seen only twice, who had hardly spoken to me, and about whom I knew nothing—absolutely nothing—but for whom I felt a tenderness and responsibility that I had never felt before?

My grandmother was not pleased with my visit after all, because I didn't stay at her place more than a couple of weeks. I felt restless and ill at ease. So I took the train back to the plains, meaning to ask further questions of the stationmaster at Deoli.

But at Deoli there was a new stationmaster. The previous man had been transferred to another post within the past week. The new man didn't know anything about the girl who sold baskets. I found the owner of the tea stall, a small, shrivelled-up man, wearing greasy clothes, and asked him if he knew anything about the girl with the baskets.

'Yes, there was such a girl here. I remember quite well,' he said. 'But she has stopped coming now.'

'Why?' I asked. 'What happened to her?'

'How should I know?' said the man. 'She was nothing to me.'

And once again I had to run for the train.

As Deoli platform receded, I decided that one day I would have to break journey there, spend a day in the town, make enquiries, and find the girl who had stolen my heart with nothing but a look from her dark, impatient eyes.

With this thought I consoled myself throughout my last term in college. I went to Dehra again in the summer and when, in the early hours of the morning, the night train drew into Deoli station, I looked up and down the platform for signs of the girl, knowing I wouldn't find her but hoping just the same.

Somehow, I couldn't bring myself to break journey at Deoli and spend a day there. (If it was all fiction or a film, I reflected, I would have got down and cleared up the mystery and reached a suitable ending to the whole thing.) I think I was afraid to do this.

I was afraid of discovering what really happened to the girl. Perhaps she was no longer in Deoli, perhaps she was married, perhaps she had fallen ill…

In the last few years I have passed through Deoli many times, and I always look out of the carriage window half expecting to see the same unchanged face smiling up at me. I wonder what happens in Deoli, behind the station walls. But I will never break my journey there. I prefer to keep hoping and dreaming and looking out of the window up and down that lonely platform, waiting for the girl with the baskets.

I never break my journey at Deoli but I pass through as often as I can.

THE VISITOR

Amir was sitting on his bed, staring out of the door that opened out onto the roof. The bald myna that was perched on the roof stared back at him. Then he heard someone calling from downstairs.

'Does anyone live up there?'

'No,' shouted Amir. 'Nobody lives up here.'

'Then can I come up?' asked the person below.

Amir didn't answer. Presently he heard footsteps coming up. The myna flew away and settled in a mango tree.

A boy stood in the doorway, smiling at Amir. He was a little taller than Amir, and much thinner. He wore a white shirt and striped pyjamas. On his feet were open slippers. A tray hung from his shoulders, filled with an assortment of goods.

'Would you like to buy something?' he asked.

In his tray were combs, buttons, reels of thread, shoelaces and little vials of cheap perfume.

'I have everything you need,' he said.

'I don't need anything,' said Amir.

'You need buttons.'

'I don't.'

'Your top button is missing.'

Amir felt for the top button of his shirt and was surprised to find it missing.

'I don't like buttoning my shirt,' he said.

'That's different,' said his visitor, and looked him up and down for further signs of wear and tear. 'You'd better buy a new pair of shoelaces.'

Amit looked down at his shoes and said, 'I've got laces.'

'Very poor quality,' said the boy and, taking hold of one of the laces, he tugged at it and snapped it in two. 'See how easily it breaks? Now you need laces.'

'Well, I'm not buying any,' said Amir.

The boy sighed, shrugged, and moved towards the door. As he walked slowly down the steps, Amir stood in the doorway watching him go. On an impulse, he called out, 'What's your name?'

'Mohan,' replied the boy.

'Well, come again in a week,' said Amir. 'I might need something then.'

~

Amir went downstairs for lunch. He returned to his room to study, but dozed off instead. Towards evening he felt hungry and restless. He could not remain in his room when everyone else was pouring into the streets to shop and talk and eat and visit the cinema.

From the roof he could see the bazaar lights coming on, and hear the jingle of tonga bells and the blare of bus horns. It was a cool evening and he put on his coat before going downstairs.

It was not easy to walk fast on the road to the bazaar. Apart from the great number of pedestrians, there were cyclists and scooter-rickshaws, handcarts and cows, all making movement difficult. A little tea shop played film music over a loudspeaker, adding noise to the general confusion.

The balloon man was having a trying time. He was surrounded by a swarm of children who were more intent on bursting his balloons than on buying any. One or two got loose and went sailing over the heads of the crowd to burst over the fire in the chaat shop.

Amir stood outside the chaat shop and ate a variety of spicy snacks. Then he wiped his fingers on the banana leaves on which he had been served, and moved on down the bazaar road.

Towards the clock tower the road grew wider and less crowded. There was a street lamp at the corner of the road. A boy was sitting on the pavement beneath the lamp, bent over a book, absorbed in what he was reading. He seemed not to notice the noise of the bazaar or the chill in the air. As Amir came nearer, he saw that the boy was Mohan.

He did not know whether to stop and talk to him, or carry on down the road. After walking some distance, he felt ashamed at not having stopped to greet the boy, so he retraced his steps. But when he came to the lamp post, Mohan had gone.

༄

When Mohan came again he did not call out from below but came straight up to the room. He looked at Amir's shirt and shoes and saw that one of the shoes was still done up with half a lace. With an air of triumph he dropped a pair of shoelaces on the desk.

'I can't pay for them now,' said Amir.

'You can pay me later.'

Amir sat on the edge of his table while Mohan leant against the wall.

'Do you go to school?' asked Amir.

'Sometimes I go to evening classes,' Mohan said. 'I am sitting for my high school exams next month. If I pass...'

He stopped to think about the things he could do if he passed. The way to a career would be open to him, he could study further, become an engineer, or a scientist or an administrator. No more selling combs and buttons at street corners...

'Where are your parents?' asked Amir.

'My father is dead. My mother is in our village in the hills. I have brothers and sisters at home, but I am the only one old enough to work.'

'Then where do you stay?'

'Anywhere. On somebody's veranda, or on the maidan; it doesn't matter much in the summer. These days I sleep on the station platform. It's quite warm there.'

'You can sleep here,' said Amir.

∽

One morning, when he opened the door of his room, Amir found Mohan asleep at the top of the steps. He had wrapped himself up in a thin blanket. His tray of merchandise lay a short distance away.

Amir shook him gently and he woke up immediately, blinking in the bright sunlight.

'Why didn't you come in?' asked Amir. 'Why didn't you let me know you were here?'

'It was late,' said Mohan. 'I did not want to wake you. Besides, it was a fine night, not too cold.'

'Someone could have stolen your things.'

Amir made Mohan promise to sleep in the room that night. He came quite early. Amir lent him a blanket, and he lay down on the floor mat and slept soundly, while Amir stayed awake worrying if his guest was comfortable enough.

Mohan came quite often, leaving early in the morning before Amir could offer him a meal. He ate at little places in the bazaar.

The high school exams were nearing, and Mohan sat up late with his books. Apart from his occasional evening classes, he received no teaching.

The exams lasted for ten days, and during this time Mohan put aside his tray of odds and ends. He did his papers with confidence. He thought he had done rather well. And when it was over, he took up his tray again and walked all over the town, trying to make up for lost sales.

∽

On the day the exams results were due, Amir rose early. He got to the news agency at five o'clock, just as the morning papers arrived. Bharu gave him a paper to look at and he found the page on which the results were listed. He looked down the 'passes' column for the town, but couldn't find Mohan's number on the list. He looked twice to make sure, and then returned the paper to Bharu with a glum look.

'Failed?' said Bharu.

Amir nodded and turned away. When he returned to the room, he found Mohan sitting at the top of the steps. He didn't have to tell him anything. Mohan knew by the look on his face.

Amir sat down beside him, and they said nothing for a while.

'Never mind,' said Mohan. 'I'll pass next year.' It seemed that Amir was more in need of comforting than himself.

'If only you'd had more time,' said Amir.

'I have plenty of time now. Another year... Can I still stay in your room?'

'For as long as it's my room. That means I shall have to work too, otherwise my grandfather will drag me downstairs again.'

Mohan laughed and went into the room. When he came out, the tray was hanging from his shoulders.

'What would you like to buy?' he asked. 'I have everything you need.'

OF RIVERS AND PILGRIMS

It's a funny thing, but long before I arrive at a place I can usually tell whether I am going to like it or not. Thus, while I was still some twenty miles from the district town of Pauri, I felt it was not going to be my sort of place, and sure enough it wasn't. A seedy, overgrown place, with too many government offices. On the other hand, while Nandprayag was still out of sight, I knew I was going to like it. And I did.

Perhaps, it's something on the wind—emanations of an atmosphere—that carry to me well before I arrive at my destination. I can't really explain it, and of course it's silly to make judgements in advance. But it does happen.

Anyway, I felt I was nearing home as soon as the bus brought me into the cheerful roadside hamlet, a little way above the Nandakini River's confluence with the Alaknanda. A prayag is a meeting place of two rivers, hence Nandprayag, the place where these two mountain rivers meet. As there are many rivers in the Garhwal Himalayas, all linking up to join either the Ganga or the Yamuna, it follows that there are numerous prayags, in themselves places of pilgrimage as well as wayside halts en route to the higher Hindu shrines at Kedarnath and Badrinath. Nowhere else in these mountains are there so many temples, sacred streams, holy places, and holy men.

Some little way above Nandprayag's sleepy little bazaar is a tourist rest house. It has a well-kept garden surrounded by fruit trees and is a little distance from the general hubbub of the main road.

Above it is the old pilgrim path. Just over twenty years ago, if you were a pilgrim intent on seeking salvation at the abode of the gods, you travelled on foot all the way from the plains, climbing about 200 miles in a couple of months. Those pilgrims had the time, the faith, and the endurance. Illness and misadventure often dogged their footsteps, but what was a little suffering if at the end of the day they arrived at the very portals of heaven?

Today's pilgrims may not be lacking in devotion, but most of them do expect to come home again.

Along the old pilgrim path are several handsome houses, set among mango trees and the fronds of the papaya and banana. Higher up the hill the pine forests commence, but down here it is almost subtropical. Nandprayag is only about 3,000 feet above sea level—a height at which the vegetation is usually lush provided there is protection from the wind.

In one of these double-storeyed houses lives Devki Nandan, a scholar and recluse. He welcomes me into his home and plies me with food till I am close to bursting. He has a great love for this little corner of Garhwal and proudly shows me his collection of cuttings of articles about the area. One is from a travelogue by Sister Nivedita—an Englishwoman, Margaret Noble, who became an interpreter of Hinduism to the West. Visiting Nandprayag in 1928, she wrote:

> Nandprayag is a place that ought to be famous for its beauty and order. For a mile or two before reaching it we had noticed the superior character of the agriculture and even some careful gardening of fruits and vegetables. The peasantry also suddenly grew handsome, not unlike the Kashmiris. The town itself is new, rebuilt since the Gohna flood, and its temple stands far out across the fields on the shore of the Prayag. But in this short time a wonderful energy has been at work on architectural carvings and the little place is full of gem-like beauties. As the road crosses

the river, I noticed two or three old Pathan tombs, the only traces of Mohammedanism that we had seen north of Srinagar in Garhwal.

Little has changed since Sister Nivedita's visit. There is still a small and thriving Pathan population in Nandprayag. In fact, when I called on Mr Nandan, he was in the act of sending out Eid greetings to his Muslim friends. Some of the old graves have disappeared in the debris from new road cuttings. As for the beautiful temple described by Sister Nivedita, I learned that it had been swept away by a mighty flood in 1970 when a cloudburst and subsequent landslide up-river resulted in great destruction downstream.

~

Mr Nandan remembers the time when he walked to the small hill station of Pauri to join the old Messmore Christian Mission School, where so many famous sons of Garhwal received their early education. It took him four days marching to get to Pauri. Now it is just four hours by bus. It was only after the Chinese invasion of 1962 that there was a sudden spurt in road building in the northern hill districts. Before that, everyone walked and thought nothing of it.

Sitting on my own that same evening in the little garden of the rest house, I heard innumerable birds break into song. I did not see them, because the light was fading and the trees were dark; but I heard the rather melancholy call of the hill dove, the ascending trill of the koel, and much shrieking, whistling, and twittering that I could not assign to any particular species.

Now, once again, while I sit on the lawn surrounded by zinnias in full bloom, I am teased by that feeling of having been here before, on this lush hillside, among the pomegranates and oleanders. Is it some childhood memory asserting itself? As far as I know, I never travelled in these parts.

It's true that Nandprayag resembles some parts of the Doon Valley (where I grew up) before the Doon was submerged by a tidal wave of humanity. But in the Doon there is no great river running past your garden. Here there are two, and they are also part of this feeling of belonging.

⁓

Presently, the room boy joins me for a chat on the lawn. He is in fact running the rest house in the absence of the manager. Wherever I go in India, the manager is usually absent; it seems to make no difference. A coach load of pilgrims is due at any moment, but until they arrive the place is empty and only the birds can be heard.

The room boy's name is Janakpal and he tells me something about his village on the next mountain, where a marauding leopard has been carrying off goats and cattle. He doesn't think much of the laws protecting leopards—nothing can be done unless the animal becomes a man-eater.

A shower of rain descends on us, and so do the pilgrims. Janakpal leaves me to attend to his duties. But I am not left alone for long. A youngster with a cup of tea is the next to interview me. He wants me to take him to Mussoorie or New Delhi. He is fed up, he says, with washing dishes here.

'You are better off here,' I tell him sincerely. 'In Mussoorie you will have twice as many dishes to wash. In Delhi, ten times as many.'

'Yes, but there are cinemas and video and TV there,' he says, leaving me without an argument. Bird song may have charms for me, but not for the restless dishwasher in tranquil Nandprayag.

The rain stops and I go for a walk. The pilgrims keep to themselves, but the locals are always ready to talk. I remember a saying (and it may have originated in these hills), which goes: 'All men are my friends. I have only to meet them.' In Nandprayag, where life still moves at a leisurely and civilized pace, one is constantly meeting them.

A GOOD PLACE FOR TREES

As my father had told me, Dehra was a good place for trees, and Grandmother's house was surrounded by several kinds—peepul, neem, mango, jackfruit, papaya and an ancient banyan tree. Some of the trees had been planted by my father and grandfather.

'How old is the jackfruit tree?' I asked Grandmother.

'Now let me see,' said Grandmother, looking very thoughtful. 'I should remember the jackfruit tree. Oh yes, your grandfather put it down in 1927. It was during the rainy season. I remember, because it was your father's birthday, and we celebrated it by planting a tree. 14 July 1927. Long before you were born!'

The banyan tree grew behind the house. Its spreading aerial roots which descended into the ground formed a number of twisting passageways in which I liked to wander. The tree was older than the house, older than my grandparents, as old as Dehra. I could hide myself among the roots, behind thick green leaves, and spy on the world below.

It was an enormous tree, about sixty feet high, and the first time I saw it I trembled with excitement because I had never seen such a marvellous tree before. I approached it slowly, even cautiously, as I wasn't sure the tree wanted my friendship. It looked as though it had many secrets. There were sounds and movement in the branches, but I couldn't see who or what made the sounds.

The tree made the first move, the first sign of friendship. It allowed a leaf to fall.

The leaf brushed against my face as it floated down but before it could reach the ground I caught and held it. I studied the leaf, running my fingers over its smooth, glossy surface. Then I put out my hand and touched the rough bark of the tree and this felt good to me. So I removed my shoes and socks, as people do when they enter a holy place, and finding first a foothold and then a handhold on that broad trunk I pulled myself up with the help of the tree's aerial roots.

As I climbed, it seemed as though someone was helping me, that invisible hands, the hands of the spirit in the tree, touched me and helped me climb.

But although the tree wanted me, there were others who were disturbed and alarmed by my arrival. A pair of parrots suddenly shot out of a hole in the trunk and, with shrill cries, flew across the garden, flashes of green and red and gold. A squirrel looked out from behind a branch, saw me, and went scurrying away to inform his friends and relatives.

I climbed higher, looked up, and saw a red beak poised above my head. I shrank away, but the hornbill made no attempt to attack me. He was relaxing in his home, which was a great hole in the tree trunk. Only the bird's head and massive beak were showing. He looked at me in a rather bored way, sleepily opening and shutting his eyes.

'So many creatures live here,' I said to myself. 'I hope none of them is dangerous!' At that moment the hornbill sprang at a passing cricket. Bill and tree trunk met with a loud and resonant 'tonk'!

I was so startled that I nearly fell off the tree. But it was a difficult tree to fall off! It was full of places where one could sit or even lie down. So I moved away from the hornbill, crawled along a branch and so moved quite a distance from the main body of the tree. I left its cold, dark depths for an area penetrated by shafts of sunlight.

No one could see me. I lay flat on the broad branch hidden by a screen of leaves. People passed by on the road below. A sahib in a sun helmet. His memsahib twirling a coloured sun umbrella. Obviously she did not want to get too brown and be mistaken for a country-born person. Behind them, a pram wheeled along by a nanny.

Then there were a number of locals, some in white dhotis, some in western clothes, some in loincloths. Some with baskets on their heads. Others with coolies to carry their baskets for them. A cloud of dust, the blare of a horn, and down the road, like an out-of-condition dragon, came the latest Morris touring car; then cyclists. Then a man with a basket of papaya balanced on his head. Following him, came a man with a performing monkey. This man rattled a little hand drum, and children followed man and monkey along the road. They stopped in the shade of a mango tree on the other side of the road. The little red monkey wore a frilled dress and a baby's bonnet. It danced for the children, while the man sang and played his drum.

The clip-clop of a tonga pony, and Bansi's tonga came rattling down the road. I called down to him, and he reined in with a shout of surprise, and looked up into the branches of the banyan tree.

'What are you doing up there?' he cried.

'Hiding from Grandmother,' I said.

'And when are you coming for that ride?'

'On Tuesday afternoon,' I said.

'Why not today?'

'Ayah won't let me. But she has Tuesdays off.'

Bansi spat red paan juice across the road. 'Your Ayah is jealous,' he said.

'I know,' I said. 'Women are always jealous, aren't they? I suppose it's because she doesn't have a tonga.'

'It's because she doesn't have a tonga driver,' said Bansi, grinning up at me. 'Never mind, I'll come on Tuesday—that's the day after tomorrow, isn't it?'

I nodded down to him, and then started backing along my branch, because I could hear Ayah calling in the distance. Bansi leant forward and smacked his pony across the rump, and the tonga shot forward.

'What are you doing up there?' asked Ayah a little later.

'I was watching a snake cross the road,' I said. I knew she couldn't resist talking about snakes. There weren't as many in Dehra as there had been in Kathiawar, and she was thrilled that I had seen one.

'Was it moving towards you or away from you?' she asked.

'It was going away.'

Ayah's face clouded over. 'That means poverty for the beholder,' she said gloomily.

Later, while scrubbing me down in the bathroom, she began to talk about her dislikes, which included drunkards ('they die quickly, anyway'), misers ('they get murdered sooner or later') and tonga drivers ('they have all the vices').

'You are a very lucky boy,' she said suddenly, peering closely at my tummy.

'Why?' I asked. 'You just said I would be poor because I saw a snake going the wrong way.'

'Well, you won't be poor for long. You have a mole on your tummy, and that's very lucky. And there is one under your armpit, which means you will be famous. Do you have one on the neck? No, thank God! A mole on the neck is the sign of a murderer!'

'Do you have any moles?' I asked.

Ayah nodded seriously, and pulling her sleeve up to her shoulder, showed me a large mole on her arm.

'What does that mean?' I asked.

'It means a life of great sadness,' said Ayah gloomily.

'Can I touch it?' I asked.

'Yes, touch it,' she said, and taking my hand she placed it against the mole.

'It's a nice mole,' I said, wanting to make Ayah happy. 'Can I kiss it?'

'You can kiss it,' said Ayah.

I kissed her on the mole.

'That's nice,' she said.

TIME STOPS AT SHAMLI

The Dehra Express usually drew into Shamli at about five o'clock in the morning at which time the station would be dimly lit and the jungle across the tracks would just be visible in the faint light of dawn. Shamli is a small station at the foot of the Shivalik Hills and the Shivaliks lie at the foot of the Himalayas, which in turn lie at the feet of God.

The station, I remember, had only one platform, an office for the stationmaster, and a waiting room. The platform boasted a tea stall, a fruit vendor, and a few stray dogs. Not much else was required because the train stopped at Shamli for only five minutes.

Why it stopped at Shamli, I never could tell. Nobody got off or on. There were never any coolies to be seen. But the train would stand there a full five minutes and the guard would blow his whistle and soon Shamli would be left behind and forgotten...until I passed that way again.

I was paying my relations in Saharanpur an annual visit when the night train stopped at Shamli. I was thirty-six at the time and still single.

On this particular journey, the train came into Shamli just as I awoke from a restless sleep. The third-class compartment was crowded beyond capacity and I had been sleeping in an upright position with my back to the lavatory door. Now someone was trying to get into the lavatory. He was obviously hard pressed for time.

'I'm sorry, brother,' I said, moving as much as I could to

one side.

He stumbled into the closet without bothering to close the door.

'Where are we now?' I asked the man sitting beside me. He was smoking a strong aromatic bidi.

'Shamli station,' he said, rubbing the palm of a large calloused hand over the frosted glass of the window.

I let the window down and stuck my head out. There was a cool breeze blowing down the platform, a breeze that whispered of autumn in the hills. As usual there was no activity except for the fruit vendor walking up and down the length of the train with his basket of mangoes balanced on his head. At the tea stall, a kettle was steaming, but there was no one to mind it. I rested my forehead on the window ledge and let the breeze play on my temples. I had been feeling sick and giddy but there was a wild sweetness in the wind that I found soothing.

'Yes,' I said to myself, 'I wonder what happens in Shamli behind the station walls.'

My fellow passenger offered me a bidi. He was a farmer, I think, on his way to Dehra. He had a long, untidy, sad moustache.

We had been more than five minutes at the station. I looked up and down the platform, but nobody was getting on or off the train. Presently the guard came walking past our compartment.

'What's the delay?' I asked him.

'Some obstruction further down the line,' he said.

'Will we be here long?'

'I don't know what the trouble is. About half an hour at the least.'

My neighbour shrugged and throwing the remains of his bidi out of the window, closed his eyes and immediately fell asleep. I moved restlessly in my seat and then the man came out of the lavatory, not so urgently now, and with obvious peace of mind. I closed the door for him.

I stood up and stretched and this stretching of my limbs

seemed to set in motion a stretching of the mind and I found myself thinking: 'I am in no hurry to get to Saharanpur and I have always wanted to see Shamli behind the station walls. If I get down now, I can spend the day here. It will be better than sitting in this train for another hour. Then in the evening I can catch the next train home.'

In those days I never had the patience to wait for second thoughts and so I began pulling my small suitcase out from under the seat.

The farmer woke up and asked, 'What are you doing, brother?'

'I'm getting out,' I said.

He went to sleep again.

It would have taken at least fifteen minutes to reach the door as people and their belongings cluttered up the passage. So I let my suitcase down from the window and followed it on to the platform.

There was no one to collect my ticket at the barrier because there was obviously no point in keeping a man there to collect tickets from passengers who never came. And anyway, I had a through-ticket to my destination which I would need in the evening.

I went out of the station and came to Shamli.

Outside the station there was a neem tree and under it stood a tonga. The pony was nibbling at the grass at the foot of the tree. The youth in the front seat was the only human in sight. There were no signs of inhabitants or habitation. I approached the tonga and the youth stared at me as though he couldn't believe his eyes.

'Where is Shamli?' I asked.

'Why, friend, this is Shamli,' he said.

I looked around again but I couldn't see any sign of life. A dusty road led past the station and disappeared into the forest.

'Does anyone live here? I asked.

'I live here,' he said with an engaging smile. He looked an

amiable, happy-go-lucky fellow. He wore a cotton tunic and dirty white pyjamas.

'Where?' I asked.

'In my tonga, of course,' he said. 'I have had this pony for five years now. I carry supplies to the hotel. But today the manager has not come to collect them. You are going to the hotel? I will take you.'

'Oh, so there's a hotel?'

'Well, friend, it is called that. And there are a few houses too and some shops, but they are all a mile from the station. If they were not a mile from here, I would be out of business.'

I felt relieved but I still had the feeling of having walked into a town consisting of one station, one pony and one man.

'You can take me,' I said. 'I'm staying till this evening.'

He heaved my suitcase into the seat beside him and I climbed in at the back of the tonga. He flicked the reins and slapped his pony on the buttocks and, with a roll and a lurch, the buggy moved off down the dusty forest road.

'What brings you here?' asked the youth.

'Nothing,' I said. 'The train was delayed. I was feeling bored. And so I got off.'

He did not believe that but he didn't question me further. The sun was reaching up over the forest but the road lay in the shadow of tall trees—eucalyptus, mango and neem.

'Not many people stay in the hotel,' he said. 'So it is cheap. You will get a room for five rupees.'

'Who is the manager?'

'Mr Satish Dayal. It is his father's property. Satish Dayal could not pass his exams or get a job so his father sent him here to look after the hotel.'

The jungle thinned out and we passed a temple, a mosque, a few small shops. There was a strong smell of burnt sugar in the air and in the distance I saw a factory chimney. That, then, was the reason for Shamli's existence. We passed a bullock cart laden with sugarcane. The road went through fields of cane and maize, and then, just as we were about to re-enter the jungle, the youth pulled his horse to a side road and the hotel came into sight.

It was a small white bungalow with a garden in the front, banana trees at the sides and an orchard of guava trees at the back. We came jingling up to the front veranda. Nobody appeared, nor was there any sign of life on the premises.

'They are all asleep,' said the youth.

I said, 'I'll sit in the veranda and wait.' I got down from the tonga and the youth dropped my case on the veranda steps. Then he stooped in front of me, smiling amiably, waiting to be paid.

'Well, how much?' I asked.

'As a friend, only one rupee.'

'That's too much,' I complained. 'This is not Delhi.'

'This is Shamli,' he said. 'I am the only tonga in Shamli. You may not pay me anything, if that is your wish. But then, I will not take you back to the station this evening. You will have to walk.'

I gave him the rupee. He had both charm and cunning, an effective combination.

'Come in the evening at about six,' I said.

'I will come,' he said with an infectious smile. 'Don't worry.' I waited till the tonga had gone around the bend in the road before walking up the veranda steps.

The doors of the house were closed and there were no bells to ring. I didn't have a watch but I judged the time to be a little past six o'clock. The hotel didn't look very impressive. The whitewash was coming off the walls and the cane chairs on the veranda were old and crooked. A stag's head was mounted over the front door but one of its glass eyes had fallen out. I had often heard hunters speak of how beautiful an animal looked before it died, but how could anyone with true love of the beautiful care for the stuffed head of an animal, grotesquely mounted, with no resemblance to its living aspect?

I felt too restless to take any of the chairs. I began pacing up and down the veranda, wondering if I should start banging on the doors. Perhaps the hotel was deserted. Perhaps the tonga driver had played a trick on me. I began to regret my impulsiveness in leaving the train. When I saw the manager I would have to invent a reason for coming to his hotel. I was good at inventing reasons. I would tell him that a friend of mine had stayed here some years ago and that I was trying to trace him. I decided that my friend would have to be a little eccentric (having chosen Shamli to live in), that he had become a recluse, shutting himself off from the world. His parents—no, his sister—for his parents would be dead—had asked me to find him if I could and, as he had last been heard of in Shamli, I had taken the opportunity to enquire after him. His name would be Major Roberts, retired.

I heard a tap running at the side of the building and walking around found a young man bathing at the tap. He was strong and well built and slapped himself on the body with great enthusiasm. He had not seen me approaching so I waited until he had finished bathing and had begun to dry himself.

'Hallo,' I said.

He turned at the sound of my voice and looked at me for a few moments with a puzzled expression. He had a round cheerful face and crisp black hair. He smiled slowly. But it was a more genuine smile than the tonga driver's. So far I had met two people in Shamli and they were both smilers. That should have cheered me, but it didn't. 'You have come to stay?' he asked in a slow, easy-going voice.

'Just for the day,' I said. 'You work here?'

'Yes, my name is Daya Ram. The manager is asleep just now but I will find a room for you.'

He pulled on his vest and pyjamas and accompanied me back to the veranda. Here he picked up my suitcase and, unlocking a side door, led me into the house. We went down a passageway. Then Daya Ram stopped at the door on the right, pushed it open and took me into a small, sunny room that had a window looking out on to the orchard. There was a bed, a desk, a couple of cane chairs, and a frayed and faded red carpet.

'Is it all right?' said Daya Ram.

'Perfectly all right.'

'They have breakfast at eight o'clock. But if you are hungry, I will make something for you now.'

'No, it's all right. Are you the cook too?'

'I do everything here.'

'Do you like it?'

'No,' he said. And then added, in a sudden burst of confidence, 'There are no women for a man like me.'

'Why don't you leave, then?'

'I will,' he said, with a doubtful look on his face. 'I will leave…'

After he had gone I shut the door and went into the bathroom to bathe. The cold water refreshed me and made me feel one with the world. After I had dried myself, I sat on the bed in front of the open window. A cool breeze, smelling of rain, came through the window and played over my body. I thought I saw a movement among the trees.

And getting closer to the window, I saw a girl on a swing. She was a small girl, all by herself, and she was swinging to and fro and singing, and her song carried faintly on the breeze.

I dressed quickly and left my room. The girl's dress was billowing in the breeze, her pigtails flying about. When she saw me approaching, she stopped swinging and stared at me. I stopped a little distance away.

'Who are you?' she asked.

'A ghost,' I replied.

'You look like one,' she said.

I decided to take this as a compliment, as I was determined to make friends. I did not smile at her because some children dislike adults who smile at them all the time.

'What's your name?' I asked.

'Kiran,' she said. 'I'm ten.'

'You are getting old.'

'Well, we all have to grow old one day. Aren't you coming any closer?'

'May I?' I asked.

'You may. You can push the swing.'

One pigtail lay across the girl's chest, the other behind her shoulder. She had a serious face and obviously felt she had responsibilities. She seemed to be in a hurry to grow up, and I suppose she had no time for anyone who treated her as a child. I pushed the swing until it went higher and higher and then I stopped pushing so that she came lower each time and we could talk.

'Tell me about the people who live here,' I said.

'There is Heera,' she said. 'He's the gardener. He's nearly a hundred. You can see him behind the hedges in the garden. You can't see him unless you look hard. He tells me stories, a new story every day. He's much better than the people in the hotel and so is Daya Ram.'

'Yes, I met Daya Ram.'

'He's my bodyguard. He brings me nice things from the kitchen when no one is looking.'

'You don't stay here?'

'No, I live in another house. You can't see it from here. My father is the manager of the factory.'

'Aren't there any other children to play with?' I asked.

'I don't know any,' she said.

'And the people staying here?'

'Oh, they.' Apparently Kiran didn't think much of the hotel guests. 'Miss Deeds is funny when she's drunk. And Mr Lin is the strangest.'

'And what about the manager, Mr Dayal?'

'He's mean. And he gets frightened of the slightest things. But Mrs Dayal is nice. She lets me take flowers home. But she doesn't talk much.'

I was fascinated by Kiran's ruthless summing up of the guests. I brought the swing to a standstill and asked, 'And what do you think of me?' 'I don't know as yet,' said Kiran quite seriously. 'I'll think about you.'

As I came back to the hotel, I heard the sound of a piano in one of the front rooms. I didn't know enough about music to be able to recognize the piece but it had sweetness and melody though it was played with some hesitancy. As I came nearer, the sweetness deserted the music, probably because the piano was out of tune.

The person at the piano had distinctive Mongolian features and so I presumed he was Mr Lin. He hadn't seen me enter the room and I stood beside the curtains of the door, watching him play. He had full round lips and high, slanting cheekbones. His eyes were large and round and full of melancholy. His long, slender fingers hardly touched the keys.

I came nearer and then he looked up at me, without any show of surprise or displeasure, and kept on playing.

'What are you playing?' I asked.

'Chopin,' he said.

'Oh, yes. It's nice but the piano is fighting it.'

'I know. This piano belonged to one of Kipling's aunts. It hasn't been tuned since the last century.'

'Do you live here?'

'No, I come from Calcutta,' he answered readily. 'I have some business here with the sugarcane people, actually, though I am not a businessman.' He was playing softly all the time so that our conversation was not lost in the music. 'I don't know anything about business. But I have to do something.'

'Where did you learn to play the piano?'

'In Singapore. A French lady taught me. She had great hopes of my becoming a concert pianist when I grew up. I would have toured Europe and America.'

'Why didn't you?'

'We left during the war and I had to give up my lessons.'

'And why did you go to Calcutta?'

'My father is a Calcutta businessman. What do you do and why do you come here?' he asked. 'If I am not being too inquisitive.'

Before I could answer, a bell rang, loud and continuously, drowning the music and conversation.

'Breakfast,' said Mr Lin.

A thin dark man, wearing glasses, stepped nervously into the room and peered at me in an anxious manner.

'You arrived last night?'

'That's right,' I said. 'I just want to stay the day. I think you're the manager?'

'Yes. Would you like to sign the register?'

I went with him past the bar and into the office. I wrote my name and Mussoorie address in the register and the duration of my stay. I paused at the column marked 'profession', thought it would be best to fill it with something and wrote 'author'.

'You are here on business?' asked Mr Dayal.

'No, not exactly. You see, I'm looking for a friend of mine who was last heard of in Shamli, about three years ago. I thought I'd make a few enquiries in case he's still here.'

'What was his name? Perhaps he stayed here.'

'Major Roberts,' I said. 'An Anglo-Indian.'

'Well, you can look through the old registers after breakfast.'

He accompanied me into the dining room. The establishment was really more of a boarding house than a hotel because Mr Dayal ate with his guests. There was a round mahogany dining table in the centre of the room and Mr Lin was the only one seated at it. Daya Ram hovered about with plates and trays. I took my seat next to Lin and, as I did so, a door opened from the passage and a woman of about thirty-five came in.

She had on a skirt and blouse which accentuated a firm, well-rounded figure, and she walked on high heels, with a rhythmical swaying of the hips. She had an uninteresting face, camouflaged with lipstick, rouge and powder—the powder so thick that it had become embedded in the natural lines of her face—but her figure compelled admiration.

'Miss Deeds,' whispered Lin.

There was a false note to her greeting.

'Hallo, everyone,' she said heartily, straining for effect. 'Why are you all so quiet? Has Mr Lin been playing the *Funeral March* again?'

She sat down and continued talking. 'Really, we must have a dance or something to liven things up. You must know some good numbers, Lin, after your experience of Singapore nightclubs. What's for breakfast? Boiled eggs. Daya Ram, can't you make an omelette for a change? I know you're not a professional cook but you don't have to give us the same thing everyday, and there's absolutely no reason why you should burn the toast. You'll have to do something about a cook, Mr Dayal.'

Then she noticed me sitting opposite her; 'Oh, hallo,' she said, genuinely surprised. She gave me a long, appraising look.

'This gentleman,' said Mr Dayal introducing me, 'is an author.'

'That's nice,' said Miss Deeds. 'Are you married?'

'No,' I said. 'Are you?'

'Funny, isn't it,' she said, without taking offence, 'no one in this house seems to be married.'

'I'm married,' said Mr Dayal.

'Oh, yes, of course,' said Miss Deeds. 'And what brings you to Shamli?' she asked, turning to me.

'I'm looking for a friend called Major Roberts.'

Lin gave an exclamation of surprise. I thought he had seen through my deception.

But another game had begun.

'I knew him,' said Lin. 'A great friend of mine.'

'Yes,' continued Lin. 'I knew him. A good chap, Major Roberts.'

Well, there I was, inventing people to suit my convenience,

and people like Mr Lin started inventing relationships with them. I was too intrigued to try and discourage him. I wanted to see how far he would go.

'When did you meet him?' asked Lin, taking the initiative.

'Oh, only about three years back, just before he disappeared. He was last heard of in Shamli.'

'Yes, I heard he was here,' said Lin. 'But he went away, when he thought his relatives had traced him. He went into the mountains near Tibet.'

'Did he?' I said, unwilling to be instructed further. 'What part of the country? I come from the hills myself. I know the Mana and Niti passes quite well. If you have any idea of exactly where he went, I think I could find him.' I had the advantage in this exchange because I was the one who had originally invented Roberts. Yet I couldn't bring myself to end his deception, probably because I felt sorry for Lin. A happy man wouldn't take the trouble of inventing friendships with people who didn't exist. He'd be too busy with friends who did.

'You've had a lonely life, Mr Lin?' I asked.

'Lonely?' said Mr Lin, with forced incredulousness. 'I'd never been lonely till I came here a month ago. When I was in Singapore...'

'You never get any letters though, do you?' asked Miss Deeds suddenly.

Lin was silent for a moment. Then he said: 'Do you?'

Miss Deeds lifted her head a little, as a horse does when it is annoyed, and I thought her pride had been hurt, but then she laughed unobtrusively and tossed her head.

'I never write letters,' she said. 'My friends gave me up as hopeless years ago. They know it's no use writing to me because they rarely get a reply. They call me the Jungle Princess.'

Mr Dayal tittered and I found it hard to suppress a smile. To cover up my smile I asked, 'You teach here?'

'Yes, I teach at the girls' school,' she said with a frown. 'But don't talk to me about teaching. I have enough of it all day.'

'You don't like teaching?' I asked.

She gave me an aggressive look. 'Should I?' she asked.

'Shouldn't you?' I said.

She paused, and then said, 'Who are you, anyway, the inspector of schools?'

'No,' said Mr Dayal who wasn't following very well, 'he's a journalist.'

'I've heard they are nosy,' said Miss Deeds.

Once again Lin interrupted to steer the conversation away from a delicate issue.

'Where's Mrs Dayal this morning?' asked Lin.

'She spent the night with our neighbours,' said Mr Dayal. 'She should be here after lunch.'

It was the first time Mrs Dayal had been mentioned. Nobody spoke either well or ill of her. I suspected that she kept her distance from the others, avoiding familiarity. I began to wonder about Mrs Dayal.

Daya Ram came in from the veranda looking worried.

'Heera's dog has disappeared,' he said. 'He thinks a leopard took it.'

Heera, the gardener, was standing respectfully outside on the veranda steps. We all hurried out to him, firing questions which he didn't try to answer.

'Yes. It's a leopard,' said Kiran appearing from behind Heera. 'It's going to come into the hotel,' she added cheerfully.

'Be quiet,' said Satish Dayal crossly.

'There are pug marks under the trees,' said Daya Ram.

Mr Dayal, who seemed to know little about leopards or pug marks, said, 'I will take a look,' and led the way to the orchard, the rest of us trailing behind in an ill-assorted procession.

There were marks on the soft earth in the orchard (they could have been a leopard's) which went in the direction of the riverbed. Mr Dayal paled a little and went hurrying back to the hotel. Heera returned to the front garden, the least excited, the most sorrowful. Everyone else was thinking of a leopard but he was thinking of the dog.

I followed him and watched him weeding the sunflower beds. His face was wrinkled like a walnut but his eyes were clear and bright. His hands were thin and bony but there was a deftness and power in the wrist and fingers and the weeds flew fast from his spade. He had cracked, parchment-like skin. I could not help thinking of the gloss and glow of Daya Ram's limbs as I had seen them when he was bathing and wondered if Heera's had once been like that and if Daya Ram's would ever be like this, and both possibilities—or were they probabilities—saddened me. Our skin, I thought, is like the leaf of a tree, young and green and shiny. Then it gets darker and heavier, sometimes spotted with disease, sometimes eaten away. Then fading, yellow and red, then falling, crumbling into dust or feeding the flames of fire. I looked at my own skin, still smooth, not coarsened by labour.

I thought of Kiran's fresh rose-tinted complexion; Miss Deeds' skin, hard and dry; Lin's pale taut skin, stretched tightly across his prominent cheeks and forehead; and Mr Dayal's grey skin growing thick hair.

And I wondered about Mrs Dayal and the kind of skin she would have.

'Did you have the dog for long?' I asked Heera.

He looked up with surprise for he had been unaware of my presence.

'Six years, sahib,' he said. 'He was not a clever dog but he was very friendly. He followed me home one day when I was coming back from the bazaar. I kept telling him to go away but he wouldn't. It was a long walk and so I began talking to him. I liked talking to him and I have always talked to him and we have understood each other. That first night, when I came home I shut the gate between us. But he stood on the other side looking at me with trusting eyes. Why did he have to look at me like that?'

'So you kept him?'

'Yes, I could never forget the way he looked at me. I shall feel lonely now because he was my only companion. My wife and son died long ago. It seems I am to stay here forever, until everyone has gone, until there are only ghosts in Shamli. Already the ghosts are here...'

I heard a light footfall behind me and turned to find Kiran. The girl stood barefoot beside the gardener and began to pull at the weeds with her toes.

'You are a lazy one,' said the old man. 'If you want to help me, sit down and use your hands.'

I looked at the girl's fair round face and in her bright eyes I saw something old and wise. And I looked into the old man's wise eyes, and saw something forever bright and young. The skin cannot change the eyes. The eyes are the true reflection of a man's age and sensibilities. Even a blind man has hidden eyes.

'I hope we find the dog,' said Kiran. 'But I would like a leopard. Nothing ever happens here.'

'Not now,' sighed Heera. 'Not now... Why, once there was a band and people danced till morning, but now...' He paused, lost in thought and then said: 'I have always been here. I was here before Shamli.'

'Before the station?'

'Before there was a station, or a factory, or a bazaar. It was a village then, and the only way to get here was by bullock cart. Then a bus service was started, then the railway lines were laid and a station built, then they started the sugar factory, and for a few years Shamli was a town. But the jungle was bigger than the town. The rains were heavy and malaria was everywhere. People didn't stay long in Shamli. Gradually, they went back into the hills. Sometimes I too wanted to go back to the hills, but what is the use when you are old and have no one left in the world except a few flowers in a troublesome garden. I had to choose between the flowers and the hills, and I chose the flowers. I am tired now, and old, but I am not tired of flowers.'

I could see that his real world was the garden; there was more variety in his flower beds than there was in the town of Shamli. Every month, every day, there were new flowers in the garden, but there were always the same people in Shamli.

I left Kiran with the old man, and returned to my room. It must have been about eleven o'clock.

I was facing the window when I heard my door being opened. Turning around, I perceived the barrel of a gun moving slowly around the edge of the door. Behind the gun was Satish Dayal, looking hot and sweaty. I didn't know what his intentions were; so, deciding it would be better to act first and reason later, I grabbed a pillow from the bed and flung it in his face. I then threw myself at his legs and brought him crashing down to the ground.

When we got up, I was holding the gun. It was an old Enfield Rifle, probably dating back to the Afghan wars, the kind that goes off at the least encouragement.

'But...but...why?' stammered the dishevelled and alarmed Mr Dayal.

'I don't know,' I said menacingly. 'Why did you come in here pointing this at me?'

'I wasn't pointing it at you. It's for the leopard.'

'Oh, so you came into my room looking for a leopard? You have, I presume, been stalking one about the hotel?' (By now I was convinced that Mr Dayal had taken leave of his senses and was hunting imaginary leopards.)

'No, no,' cried the distraught man, becoming more confused.

'I was looking for you. I wanted to ask you if you could use a gun. I was thinking we should go looking for the leopard that took Heera's dog. Neither Mr Lin nor I can shoot.'

'Your gun is not up to date,' I said. 'It's not at all suitable for hunting leopards. A stout stick would be more effective. Why don't we arm ourselves with lathis and make a general assault?'

I said this banteringly, but Mr Dayal took the idea quite seriously. 'Yes, yes,' he said with alacrity, 'Daya Ram has got one or two lathis in the godown. The three of us could make an expedition. I have asked Mr Lin but he says he doesn't want to have anything to do with leopards.'

'What about our Jungle Princess?' I said. 'Miss Deeds should be pretty good with a lathi.'

'Yes, yes,' said Mr Dayal humourlessly, 'but we'd better not ask her.'

Collecting Daya Ram and two lathis, we set off for the orchard and began following the pug marks through the trees. It took us ten minutes to reach the riverbed, a dry, hot, rocky place; then we went into the jungle, Mr Dayal keeping well to the rear. The atmosphere was heavy and humid, and there was not a breath of air amongst the trees. When a parrot squawked suddenly, shattering the silence, Mr Dayal let out a startled exclamation and started for home.

'What was that?' he asked nervously.

'A bird,' I explained.

'I think we should go back now,' he said. 'I don't think the leopard's here.'

'You never know with leopards,' I said, 'they could be anywhere.'

Mr Dayal stepped away from the bushes. 'I'll have to go,' he said. 'I have a lot of work. You keep a lathi with you, and I'll send Daya Ram back later.'

'That's very thoughtful of you,' I said.

Daya Ram scratched his head and reluctantly followed his employer back through the trees. I moved on slowly, down the little used path, wondering if I should also return. I saw two monkeys playing on the branch of a tree, and decided that there could be no danger in the immediate vicinity.

Presently I came to a clearing where there was a pool of

fresh clear water. It was fed by a small stream that came suddenly, like a snake, out of the long grass. The water looked cool and inviting. Laying down the lathi and taking off my clothes, I ran down the bank until I was waist deep in the middle of the pool. I splashed about for some time before emerging, then I lay on the soft grass and allowed the sun to dry my body. I closed my eyes and gave myself up to beautiful thoughts. I had forgotten all about leopards.

I must have slept for about half an hour because when I awoke, I found that Daya Ram had come back and was vigorously threshing about in the narrow confines of the pool. I sat up and asked him the time.

'Twelve o'clock,' he shouted, coming out of the water, his dripping body all gold and silver in sunlight. 'They will be waiting for dinner.'

'Let them wait,' I said.

It was a relief to talk to Daya Ram, after the uneasy conversations in the lounge and dining room.

'Dayal sahib will be angry with me.'

'I'll tell him we found the trail of the leopard, and that we went so far into the jungle that we lost our way. As Miss Deeds is so critical of the food, let her cook the meal.'

'Oh, she only talks like that,' said Daya Ram. 'Inside she is very soft. She is too soft in some ways.'

'She should be married.'

'Well, she would like to be. Only there is no one to marry her. When she came here she was engaged to be married to an English army captain. I think she loved him, but she is the sort of person who cannot help loving many men all at once, and the captain could not understand that—it is just the way she is made, I suppose. She is always ready to fall in love.'

'You seem to know,' I said.

'Oh, yes.'

We dressed and walked back to the hotel. In a few hours,

I thought, the tonga will come for me and I will be back at the station. The mysterious charm of Shamli will be no more, but whenever I pass this way I will wonder about these people, about Miss Deeds and Lin and Mrs Dayal.

Mrs Dayal... She was the one person I had yet to meet. It was with some excitement and curiosity that I looked forward to meeting her; she was about the only mystery left in Shamli now, and perhaps she would be no mystery when I met her. And, yet... I felt that perhaps she would justify the impulse that made me get down from the train.

I could have asked Daya Ram about Mrs Dayal, and so satisfied my curiosity, but I wanted to discover her for myself. Half the day was left to me, and I didn't want my game to finish too early.

I walked towards the veranda, and the sound of the piano came through the open door.

'I wish Mr Lin would play something cheerful,' said Miss Deeds. 'He's obsessed with the *Funeral March*. Do you dance?'

'Oh, no,' I said.

She looked disappointed. But when Lin left the piano, she went into the lounge and sat down on the stool. I stood at the door watching her, wondering what she would do. Lin left the room somewhat resentfully.

She began to play an old song which I remembered having heard in a film or on a gramophone record. She sang while she played, in a slightly harsh but pleasant voice:

Rolling round the world
Looking for the sunshine
I know I'm gonna to find some day...

Then she played 'Am I Blue?' and 'Darling, Je Vous Aime Beaucoup'. She sat there singing in a deep, husky voice, her eyes a little misty, her hard face suddenly kind and sloppy. When the dinner gong rang, she broke off playing and shook off her sentimental mood, and laughed derisively at herself.

I don't remember that lunch. I hadn't slept much since the previous night and I was beginning to feel the strain of my journey. The swim had refreshed me, but it had also made me drowsy. I ate quite well, though, of rice and kofta curry, and then feeling sleepy, made for the garden to find a shady tree.

There were some books on the shelf in the lounge, and I ran my eye over them in search of one that might condition sleep. But they were too dull to do even that. So I went into the garden, and there was Kiran on the swing, and I went to her tree and sat down on the grass.

'Did you find the leopard?' she asked.

'No,' I said, with a yawn.

'Tell me a story.'

'You tell me one,' I said.

'All right. Once there was a lazy man with long legs, who was always yawning and wanting to fall asleep...'

I watched the swaying motions of the swing and the movements of the girl's bare legs, and a tiny insect kept buzzing about in front of my nose...

'...and fall asleep, and the reason for this was that he liked to dream.'

I blew the insect away, and the swing became hazy and distant, and Kiran was a blurred figure in the trees...

'...liked to dream, and what do you think he dreamt about..?'

Dreamt about, dreamt about...

When I awoke there was that cool, rain-scented breeze blowing across the garden. I remember lying on the grass with my eyes closed, listening to the swishing of the swing. Either I had not slept long, or Kiran had been a long time on the swing; it was moving slowly now, in a more leisurely fashion, without much sound. I opened my eyes and saw that my arm was stained with the juice of the grass beneath me. Looking up, I expected to see Kiran's legs waving above me. But instead I saw dark slim feet and above them the folds of a sari. I straightened up against the trunk of the tree to look closer at Kiran, but Kiran wasn't there. It was someone else on the swing, a young woman in a pink sari, with a red rose in her hair.

She had stopped the swing with her foot on the ground, and she was smiling at me.

It wasn't a smile you could see, it was a tender, fleeting movement that came suddenly and was gone at the same time, and its going was sad. I thought of the others' smiles, just as I had thought of their skins—the tonga driver's friendly, deceptive smile; Daya Ram's wide, sincere smile; Miss Deeds's cynical, derisive smile. And looking at Sushila, I knew a smile could never change. She had always smiled that way.

'You haven't changed,' she said.

I was standing up now, though still leaning against the tree for support. Though I had never thought much about the sound of her voice, it seemed as familiar as the sounds of yesterday.

'You haven't changed either,' I said. 'But where did you come from?'

I wasn't sure yet if I was awake or dreaming.

She laughed as she had always laughed at me.

'I came from behind the tree. The little girl has gone.'

'Yes, I'm dreaming,' I said helplessly.

'But what brings you here?'

'I don't know. At least I didn't know when I came. But it must have been you. The train stopped at Shamli and I don't know why, but I decided I would spend the day here, behind the station walls. You must be married now, Sushila.'

'Yes, I am married to Mr Dayal, the manager of the hotel. And what has been happening to you?'

'I am still a writer, still poor, and still living in Mussoorie.'

'When were you last in Delhi?' she asked. 'I don't mean Delhi, I mean at home.'

'I have not been to your home since you were there.'

'Oh, my friend,' she said, getting up suddenly and coming to me, 'I want to talk about our home and Sunil and our friends and all those things that are so far away now. I have been here two years, and I am already feeling old. I keep remembering our home—how young I was, how happy—and I am all alone with memories. But now you are here! It was a bit of magic. I came through the trees after Kiran had gone, and there you were, fast asleep under the tree. I didn't wake you because I wanted to see you wake up.'

'As I used to watch you wake up...'

She was near me and I could look at her more closely. Her cheeks did not have the same freshness—they were a little pale—and she was thinner now, but her eyes were the same, smiling the same way. Her fingers, when she took my hand, were the same warm, delicate fingers.

'Talk to me,' she said. 'Tell me about yourself.'

'You tell me,' I said.

'I am here,' she said. 'That is all there is to say about myself.'

'Then let us sit down and I'll talk.'

'Not here,' she said and took my hand and led me through the trees. 'Come with me.'

I heard the jingle of a tonga bell and a faint shout. I stopped and laughed.

'My tonga,' I said. 'It has come to take me back to the station.'

'But you are not going,' said Sushila, immediately downcast.

'I will tell him to come in the morning,' I said. 'I will spend the night in your Shamli.'

I walked to the front of the hotel where the tonga was waiting. I was glad no one else was in sight. The youth was smiling at me in his most appealing manner.

'I'm not going today,' I said. 'Will you come tomorrow morning?'

'I can come whenever you like, friend. But you will have to pay for every trip, because it is a long way from the station even if my tonga is empty. Usual fare, friend, one rupee.'

I didn't try to argue but resignedly gave him the rupee. He cracked his whip and pulled on the reins, and the carriage moved off.

'If you don't leave tomorrow,' the youth called out after me, 'you'll never leave Shamli!'

I walked back through the trees, but I couldn't find Sushila.

'Sushila, where are you?' I called, but I might have been speaking to the trees, for I had no reply. There was a small path going through the orchard, and on the path I saw a rose petal. I walked a little further and saw another petal. They were from Sushila's red rose. I walked on down the path until I had skirted the orchard, and then the path went along the fringe of the jungle, past a clump of bamboos, and here the grass was a lush green as though it had been constantly watered. I was still finding rose petals. I heard the chatter of the seven sisters, and the call of a hoopoe. The path bent to meet a stream, there was a willow coming down to the water's edge, and Sushila was waiting there.

'Why didn't you wait?' I said.

'I wanted to see if you were as good at following me as you used to be.'

'Well, I am,' I said, sitting down beside her on the grassy bank of the stream. 'Even if I'm out of practice.'

'Yes, I remember the time you climbed up an apple tree to pick some fruit for me. You got up all right but then you couldn't come down again. I had to climb up myself and help you.'

'I don't remember that,' I said.

'Of course you do.'

'It must have been your other friend, Pramod.'

'I never climbed trees with Pramod.'

'Well, I don't remember.'

I looked at the little stream that ran past us. The water was no more than ankle-deep, cold and clear and sparkling, like the mountain stream near my home. I took off my shoes, rolled up my trousers, and put my feet in the water. Sushila's feet joined mine.

At first I had wanted to ask about her marriage, whether she was happy or not, what she thought of her husband; but now I couldn't ask her these things. They seemed far away and of little importance. I could think of nothing she had in common with Mr Dayal. I felt that her charm and attractiveness and warmth could not have been appreciated, or even noticed, by that curiously distracted man. He was much older than her, of course, probably older than me. He was obviously not her choice but her parents', and so far they were childless. Had there been children, I don't think Sushila would have minded Mr Dayal as her husband. Children would have made up for the absence of passion—or was there passion in Satish Dayal? I remembered having heard that Sushila had been married to a man she didn't like. I remembered having shrugged off the news, because it meant she would never come my way again, and I have never yearned after something that has been irredeemably lost. But she had come my way again. And was she still lost? That was what I wanted to know.

'What do you do with yourself all day?' I asked.

'Oh, I visit the school and help with the classes. It is the only interest I have in this place. The hotel is terrible. I try to keep away from it as much as I can.'

'And what about the guests?'

'Oh, don't let us talk about them. Let us talk about ourselves. Do you have to go tomorrow?'

'Yes, I suppose so. Will you always be in this place?'

'I suppose so.'

That made me silent. I took her hand, and my feet churned up the mud at the bottom of the stream. As the mud subsided, I saw Sushila's face reflected in the water, and looking up at her again, into her dark eyes, the old yearning returned and I wanted to care for her and protect her. I wanted to take her away from this place, from sorrowful Shamli. I wanted her to live again.

Of course, I had forgotten all about my poor finances, Sushila's family, and the shoes I wore, which were my last pair. The uplift I was experiencing in this meeting with Sushila, who had always, throughout her childhood and youth, bewitched me as no other had ever bewitched me, made me reckless and impulsive.

I lifted her hand to my lips and kissed her on the soft of her palm.

'Can I kiss you?' I said.

'You have just done so.'

'Can I kiss you?' I repeated.

'It is not necessary.'

I leaned over and kissed her slender neck. I knew she would like this, because that was where I had kissed her often before. I kissed her on the soft of the throat, where it tickled.

'It is not necessary,' she said, but she ran her fingers through my hair and let them rest there. I kissed her behind the ear then, and kept my mouth to her ear and whispered, 'Can I kiss you?'

She turned her face to me so that we looked deep into each other's eyes, and I kissed her again. And we put our arms around each other and lay together on the grass with the water running over our feet. We said nothing at all, simply lay there for what seemed like several years, or until the first drop of rain.

It was a big wet drop, and it splashed on Sushila's cheek just next to mine, and ran down to her lips so that I had to kiss her again. The next big drop splattered on the tip of my nose, and Sushila laughed and sat up. Little ringlets were forming on the stream where the raindrops hit the water, and above us there was a pattering on the banana leaves.

'We must go,' said Sushila.

We started homewards, but had not gone far before it was raining steadily, and Sushila's hair came loose and streamed down her body. The rain fell harder, and we had to hop over pools and avoid the soft mud. Sushila's sari was plastered to her body, accentuating her ripe, thrusting breasts, and I was excited to passion. I pulled her beneath a big tree, crushed her in my arms and kissed her rain-kissed mouth. And then I thought she was crying, but I wasn't sure, because it might have been the raindrops on her cheeks.

'Come away with me,' I said. 'Leave this place. Come away with me tomorrow morning. We will go somewhere where nobody will know us or come between us.'

She smiled at me and said, 'You are still a dreamer, aren't you?'

'Why can't you come?'

'I am married. It is as simple as that.'

'If it is that simple you can come.'

'I have to think of my parents, too. It would break my father's heart if I were to do what you are proposing. And you are proposing it without a thought for the consequences.'

'You are too practical,' I said.

'If women were not practical, most marriages would be failures.'

'So your marriage is a success?'

'Of course it is, as a marriage. I am not happy and I do not love him, but neither am I so unhappy that I should hate him. Sometimes, for our own sakes, we have to think of the happiness of others. What happiness would we have living in hiding from everyone we once knew and cared for. Don't be a fool. I am always here and you can come to see me, and nobody will be made unhappy by it. But take me away and we will only have regrets.'

'You don't love me,' I said foolishly.

'That sad word love,' she said, and became pensive and silent.

I could say no more. I was angry again and rebellious, and there was no one and nothing to rebel against. I could not understand someone who was afraid to break away from an unhappy existence lest that existence should become unhappier. I had always considered it an admirable thing to break away from security and respectability. Of course, it is easier for a man to do this. A man can look after himself, he can do without neighbours and the approval of the local society. A woman, I reasoned, would do anything for love provided it was not at the price of security; for a woman loves security as much as a man loves independence.

'I must go back now,' said Sushila. 'You follow a little later.'

'All you wanted to do was talk,' I complained.

She laughed at that and pulled me playfully by the hair. Then she ran out from under the tree, springing across the grass, and the wet mud flew up and flecked her legs. I watched her through the thin curtain of rain until she reached the veranda. She turned to wave to me, and then skipped into the hotel.

The rain had lessened, but I didn't know what to do with myself. The hotel was uninviting, and it was too late to leave Shamli. If the grass hadn't been wet I would have preferred to sleep under a tree rather than return to the hotel to sit at that alarming dining table.

I came out from under the trees and crossed the garden. But instead of making for the veranda I went around to the back of the hotel. Smoke issuing from the barred window of a back room told me I had probably found the kitchen. Daya Ram was inside, squatting in front of a stove, stirring a pot of stew. The stew smelt appetizing. Daya Ram looked up and smiled at me.

'I thought you had gone,' he said.

'I'll go in the morning,' I said, pulling myself up on an empty table. Then I had one of my sudden ideas and said, 'Why don't you come with me? I can find you a good job in Mussoorie. How much do you get paid here?'

'Fifty rupees a month. But I haven't been paid for three months.'

'Could you get your pay before tomorrow morning?'

'No, I won't get anything until one of the guests pays a bill. Miss Deeds owes about fifty rupees on whisky alone. She will pay up, she says, when the school pays her salary. And the school can't pay her until they collect the children's fees. That is how bankrupt everyone is in Shamli.'

'I see,' I said, though I didn't see. 'But Mr Dayal can't hold back your pay just because his guests haven't paid their bills.'

'He can if he hasn't got any money.'

'I see,' I said. 'Anyway, I will give you my address. You can come when you are free.'

'I will take it from the register,' he said.

I edged over to the stove and leaning over, sniffed at the stew.

'I'll eat mine now,' I said. And without giving Daya Ram a chance to object, I lifted a plate off the shelf, took hold of the stirring spoon and helped myself from the pot.

'There's rice too,' said Daya Ram.

I filled another plate with rice and then got busy with my fingers. After ten minutes I had finished. I sat back comfortably, in a ruminative mood. With my stomach full I could take a more tolerant view of life and people. I could understand Sushila's apprehensions, Lin's delicate lying and Miss Deeds's aggressiveness. Daya Ram went out to sound the dinner gong, and I trailed back to my room.

From the window of my room I saw Kiran running across the lawn and I called to her, but she didn't hear me. She ran down the path and out of the gate, her pigtails beating against the wind.

The clouds were breaking and coming together again, twisting and spiralling their way across a violet sky. The sun was going down behind the Shivaliks. The sky there was bloodshot. The tall slim trunks of the eucalyptus trees were tinged with an orange glow; the rain had stopped, and the wind was a soft, sullen puff, drifting sadly through the trees. There was a steady drip of water from the eaves of the roof on to the window sill. Then the sun went down behind the old, old hills, and I remembered my own hills, far beyond these.

The room was dark but I did not turn on the light. I

stood near the window, listening to the garden. There was a frog warbling somewhere and there was a sudden flap of wings overhead. Tomorrow morning I would go, and perhaps I would come back to Shamli one day, and perhaps not. I could always come here looking for Major Roberts, and who knows, one day I might find him. What should he be like, this lost man? A romantic, a man with a dream, a man with brown skin and blue eyes, living in a hut on a snowy mountain top, chopping wood and catching fish and swimming in cold mountain streams; a rough, free man with a kind heart and a shaggy beard, a man who owed allegiance to no one, who gave a damn for money and politics, and cities and civilizations, who was his own master, who lived at one with nature knowing no fear. But that was not Major Roberts—that was the man I wanted to be. He was not a Frenchman or an Englishman, he was me, a dream of myself. If only I could find Major Roberts.

When Daya Ram knocked on the door and told me the others had finished dinner, I left my room and made for the lounge. It was quite lively in the lounge. Satish Dayal was at the bar, Lin at the piano, and Miss Deeds in the middle of the room executing a tango on her own. It was obvious she had been drinking heavily.

'All on credit,' complained Mr Dayal to me. 'I don't know when I'll be paid, but I don't dare refuse her anything for fear she starts breaking up the hotel.'

'She could do that, too,' I said. 'It would come down without much encouragement.'

Lin began to play a waltz (I think it was a waltz), and then I found Miss Deeds in front of me, saying, 'Wouldn't you like to dance, old boy?'

'Thank you,' I said, somewhat alarmed. 'I hardly know how to.'

'Oh, come on, be a sport,' she said, pulling me away from the bar. I was glad Sushila wasn't present. She wouldn't have minded, but she'd have laughed as she always laughed when I made a fool of myself.

We went around the floor in what I suppose was waltz time, though all I did was mark time to Miss Deeds's motions. We were not very steady—this because I was trying to keep her at arm's length, while she was determined to have me crushed to her bosom. At length Lin finished the waltz. Giving him a grateful look, I pulled myself free. Miss Deeds went over to the piano, leaned right across it, and said, 'Play something lively, dear Mr Lin, play some hot stuff.'

To my surprise, Mr Lin without so much as an expression of distaste or amusement, began to execute what I suppose was the frug or the jitterbug. I was glad she hadn't asked me to dance that one with her.

It all appeared very incongruous to me—Miss Deeds letting herself go in crazy abandonment, Lin playing the piano with great seriousness, and Mr Dayal watching from the bar with an anxious frown. I wondered what Sushila would have thought of them now.

Eventually, Miss Deeds collapsed on the couch breathing heavily.

'Give me a drink,' she cried.

With the noblest of intentions I took her a glass of water. Miss Deeds took a sip and made a face. 'What's this stuff?' she asked. 'It is different.'

'Water,' I said.

'No,' she said, 'now don't joke, tell me what it is.'

'It's water, I assure you,' I said.

When she saw that I was serious, her face coloured up and I thought she would throw the water at me. But she was too tired to do this and contented herself with throwing the glass over her shoulder. Mr Dayal made a dive for the flying glass, but he wasn't in time to rescue it and it hit the wall and fell to pieces on the floor.

Mr Dayal wrung his hands. 'You'd better take her to her

room,' he said, as though I were personally responsible for her behaviour just because I'd danced with her.

'I can't carry her alone,' I said, making an unsuccessful attempt at helping Miss Deeds up from the couch.

Mr Dayal called for Daya Ram, and the big amiable youth came lumbering into the lounge. We took an arm each and helped Miss Deeds, feet dragging, across the room. We got her to her room and on to her bed. When we were about to withdraw she said, 'Don't go, my dear, stay with me a little while.'

Daya Ram had discreetly slipped outside. With my hand on the doorknob I said, 'Which of us?'

'Oh, are there two of you?' said Miss Deeds, without a trace of disappointment.

'Yes, Daya Ram helped me carry you here.'

'Oh, and who are you?'

'I'm the writer. You danced with me, remember?'

'Of course. You dance divinely, Mr Writer. Do stay with me. Daya Ram can stay too if he likes.'

I hesitated, my hand on the doorknob. She hadn't opened her eyes all the time I'd been in the room, her arms hung loose, and one bare leg hung over the side of the bed. She was fascinating somehow, and desirable, but I was afraid of her. I went out of the room and quietly closed the door.

As I lay awake in bed I heard the jackal's 'pheau', the cry of fear which it communicates to all the jungle when there is danger about, a leopard or a tiger. It was a weird howl, and between each note there was a kind of low gurgling. I switched off the light and peered through the closed window. I saw the jackal at the edge of the lawn. It sat almost vertically on its haunches, holding its head straight up to the sky, making the neighbourhood vibrate with the eerie violence of its cries. Then suddenly it started up and ran off into the trees.

Before getting back into bed I made sure the window was shut. The bullfrog was singing again, 'ing-ong, ing-ong', in some foreign language. I wondered if Sushila was awake too, thinking about me. It must have been almost eleven o'clock. I thought of Miss Deeds with her leg hanging over the edge of the bed. I tossed restlessly and then sat up. I hadn't slept for two nights but I was not sleepy. I got out of bed without turning on the light and slowly opening my door, crept down the passageway. I stopped at the door of Miss Deeds's room. I stood there listening, but I heard only the ticking of the big clock that might have been in the room or somewhere in the passage. I put my hand on the doorknob but the door was bolted. That settled the matter.

I would definitely leave Shamli the next morning. Another day in the company of these people and I would be behaving like them. Perhaps I was already doing so! I remembered the tonga driver's words: 'Don't stay too long in Shamli or you will never leave!'

When the rain came, it was not with a preliminary patter or shower, but all at once, sweeping across the forest like a massive wall, and I could hear it in the trees long before it reached the house. Then it came crashing down on the corrugated roof, and the hailstones hit the windowpanes with a hard metallic sound so that I thought the glass would break. The sound of thunder was like the booming of big guns and the lightning kept playing over the garden. At every flash of lightning I sighted the swing under the tree, rocking and leaping in the air as though some invisible, agitated being was sitting on it. I wondered about Kiran. Was she sleeping through all this, blissfully unconcerned, or was she lying awake in bed, starting at every clash of thunder as I was? Or was she up and about, exulting in the storm? I half expected to see her come running through the trees, through the rain, to stand on the swing with her hair blowing wild in the wind, laughing at the thunder and the angry skies. Perhaps I did see her, perhaps she was there. I wouldn't have been surprised if she were some forest nymph living in the hole of a tree, coming out sometimes to play in the garden.

A crash, nearer and louder than any thunder so far, made me sit up in bed with a start. Perhaps lightning had struck the house. I turned on the switch but the light didn't come on. A tree must have fallen across the line.

I heard voices in the passage—the voices of several people. I stepped outside to find out what had happened, and started at the appearance of a ghostly apparition right in front of me. It was Mr Dayal standing on the threshold in an oversized pyjama suit, a candle in his hand.

'I came to wake you,' he said. 'This storm...'

He had the irritating habit of stating the obvious.

'Yes, the storm,' I said. 'Why is everybody up?'

'The back wall has collapsed and part of the roof has fallen in. We'd better spend the night in the lounge—it is the safest room. This is a very old building,' he added apologetically.

'All right,' I said. 'I am coming.'

The lounge was lit by two candles. One stood over the piano, the other on a small table near the couch. Miss Deeds was on the couch, Lin was at the piano stool, looking as though he would start playing Stravinsky any moment, and Dayal was fussing about the room. Sushila was standing at a window, looking out at the stormy night. I went to the window and touched her but she didn't look around or say anything. The lightning flashed and her dark eyes were pools of smouldering fire.

'What time will you be leaving?' she asked.

'The tonga will come for me at seven.'

'If I come,' she said, 'if I come with you, I will be at the station before the train leaves.'

'How will you get there?' I asked, and hope and excitement rushed over me again.

'I will get there,' she said. 'I will get there before you. But if I am not there, then do not wait, do not come back for me. Go on your way. It will mean I do not want to come. Or I will be there.'

'But are you sure?'

'Don't stand near me now. Don't speak to me unless you have to.' She squeezed my fingers, then drew her hand away. I sauntered over to the next window, then back into the centre of the room.

A gust of wind blew through a cracked windowpane and put out the candle near the couch.

'Damn the wind,' said Miss Deeds.

The window in my room had burst open during the night and there were leaves and branches strewn about the floor. I sat down on the damp bed and smelt eucalyptus. The earth was red, as though the storm had bled it all night.

After a little while I went into the veranda with my suitcase to wait for the tonga. It was then that I saw Kiran under the trees. Kiran's long black pigtails were tied up in a red ribbon, and she looked fresh and clean like the rain and the red earth. She stood looking seriously at me.

'Did you like the storm?' she asked.

'Some of the time,' I said. 'I'm going soon. Can I do anything for you?'

'Where are you going?'

'I'm going to the end of the world. I'm looking for Major Roberts, have you seen him anywhere?'

'There is no Major Roberts,' she said perceptively. 'Can I come with you to the end of the world?'

'What about your parents?'

'Oh, we won't take them.'

'They might be annoyed if you go off on your own.'

'I can stay on my own. I can go anywhere.'

'Well, one day I'll come back here and I'll take you everywhere and no one will stop us. Now is there anything else I can do for you?'

'I want some flowers, but I can't reach them,' she pointed to a hibiscus tree that grew against the wall. It meant climbing the wall to reach the flowers. Some of the red flowers had fallen during the night and were floating in a pool of water.

'All right,' I said, and pulled myself up on the wall. I smiled down into Kiran's serious, upturned face. 'I'll throw them to you and you can catch them.'

I bent a branch, but the wood was young and green and I had to twist it several times before it snapped.

'I hope nobody minds,' I said, as I dropped the flowering branch to Kiran.

'It's nobody's tree,' she said.

'Sure?'

She nodded vigorously. 'Sure, don't worry.'

I was working for her and she felt immensely capable of protecting me. Talking and being with Kiran, I felt a nostalgic longing for childhood—emotions that had been beautiful because they were never completely understood.

'Who is your best friend?' I said.

'Daya Ram,' she replied. 'I told you so before.'

She was certainly faithful to her friends.

'And who is the second best?'

She put her finger in her mouth to consider the question, and her head dropped sideways.

'I'll make you the second best,' she said.

I dropped the flowers over her head. 'That is so kind of you. I'm proud to be your second best.'

I heard the tonga bell, and from my perch on the wall saw the carriage coming down the driveway. 'That's for me,' I said. 'I must go now.'

I jumped down the wall. And the sole of my shoe came off at last.

'I knew that would happen,' I said.

'Who cares for shoes,' said Kiran.

'Who cares,' I said.

I walked back to the veranda and Kiran walked beside me, and stood in front of the hotel while I put my suitcase in the tonga.

'You nearly stayed one day too late,' said the tonga driver. 'Half the hotel has come down and tonight the other half will come down.'

I climbed into the back seat. Kiran stood on the path, gazing intently at me.

'I'll see you again,' I said.

'I'll see you in Iceland or Japan,' she said. 'I'm going everywhere.'

'Maybe,' I said, 'maybe you will.'

We smiled, knowing and understanding each other's importance. In her bright eyes I saw something old and wise. The tonga driver cracked his whip, the wheels creaked, the carriage rattled down the path. We kept waving to each other. In Kiran's hand was a sprig of hibiscus. As she waved, the blossoms fell apart and danced a little in the breeze.

Shamli station looked the same as it had the day before. The same train stood at the same platform and the same dogs prowled beside the fence. I waited on the platform till the bell clanged for the train to leave, but Sushila did not come.

Somehow, I was not disappointed. I had never really expected her to come. Unattainable, Sushila would always be more bewitching and beautiful than if she were mine.

Shamli would always be there. And I could always come back, looking for Major Roberts.

BUS STOP, PIPALNAGAR

I

My balcony was my window on the world.

The room itself had only one window, a square hole in the wall crossed by two iron bars. The view from it was rather restricted. If I craned my neck sideways, and put my nose to the bars, I could see the end of the building. Below was a narrow courtyard where children played. Across the courtyard, on a level with my room, were three separate windows belonging to three separate rooms, each window barred in the same way, with iron bars. During the day it was difficult to see into these rooms. The harsh, cruel sunlight filled the courtyard, making the windows patches of darkness.

My room was very small. I had paced about in it so often that I knew its exact measurements. My foot, from heel to toe, was eleven inches long. That made my room just over fifteen feet in length; for, when I measured the last foot, my toes turned up against the wall. It wasn't more than eight feet broad, which meant that two people was the most it could comfortably accommodate. I was the only tenant but at times I had put up at least three friends—two on the floor, two on the bed. The plaster had been peeling off the walls and in addition the greasy stains and patches were difficult to hide, though I covered the worst ones with pictures cut out from magazines—Waheeda Rehman, the Indian actress, successfully blotted out one big patch and a recent Mr Universe displayed his muscles from the opposite wall. The biggest stain was all but concealed by a calendar that showed Ganesh, the elephant-headed god, whose blessings were vital to all good beginnings.

My belongings were few. A shelf on the wall supported an untidy pile of paperbacks, and a small table in one corner of the room supported the solid weight of my rejected manuscripts and an ancient typewriter which I had obtained on hire.

I was eighteen years old and a writer.

Such a combination would be disastrous enough anywhere, but in India it was doubly so; for there were not many papers to write for and payments were small. In addition, I was very inexperienced and though what I wrote came from the heart, only a fraction touched the hearts of editors. Nevertheless, I persevered and was able to earn about a hundred rupees a month, barely enough to keep body, soul and typewriter together. There wasn't much else I could do. Without that passport to a job—a university degree—I had no alternative but to accept the classification of 'self-employed'—which was impressive as it included doctors, lawyers, property dealers, and grain merchants, most of whom earned well over a thousand rupees a month.

'Haven't you realized that India is bursting with young people trying to pass exams?' asked a journalist friend. 'It's a desperate matter, this race for academic qualifications. Everyone wants to pass his exam the easy way, without reading too many books or attending more than half-a-dozen lectures. That's where a smart fellow like you comes in! Why would students wade through five volumes of political history when they can buy a few model answer papers at any bookstall? They are helpful, these guess papers. You can write them quickly and flood the market. They'll sell like hot cakes!'

'Who eats hot cakes here?'

'Well, then, hot chapattis.'

'I'll think about it,' I said; but the idea repelled me. If I was going to misguide students, I would rather do it by writing second-rate detective stories than by providing them with readymade answer papers. Besides, I thought it would bore me.

II

The string of the cot needed tightening. The dip in the middle of the bed was so bad that I woke up in the morning with a stiff back. But I was hopeless at tightening bed-strings and would have to wait until one of the boys from the tea shop paid me a visit. I was too tall for the cot, anyway, and if my feet didn't stick out at one end, my head lolled over the other.

Under the cot was my tin trunk. Apart from my clothes, it contained notebooks, diaries, photographs, scrapbooks, and other odds and ends that form a part of a writer's existence.

I did not live entirely alone. During cold or rainy weather, the boys from the tea shop, who normally slept on the pavement, crowded into the room. Apart from them, there were lizards on the walls and ceilings—friends these—and a large rat—definitely an enemy—who got in and out of the window and who sometimes carried away manuscripts and clothing.

June nights were the most uncomfortable. Mosquitoes emerged from all the ditches, gullies and ponds, to swarm over Pipalnagar. Bugs, finding it uncomfortable inside the woodwork of the cot, scrambled out at night and found their way under the sheet. The lizards wandered listlessly over the walls, impatient for the monsoon rains, when they would be able to feast off thousands of insects.

Everyone in Pipalnagar was waiting for the cool, quenching relief of the monsoon.

III

I woke every morning at five as soon as the first bus moved out of the shed, situated only twenty or thirty yards down the road. I dressed, went down to the tea shop for a glass of hot tea and some buttered toast, and then visited Deep Chand the barber in his shop.

At eighteen, I shaved about three times a week. Sometimes I shaved myself. But often, when I felt lazy, Deep Chand shaved me, at the special concessional rate of two annas.

'Give my head a good massage, Deep Chand,' I said. 'My brain is not functioning these days. In my latest story there are three murders, but it is boring just the same.'

'You must write a good book,' said Deep Chand, beginning the ritual of the head massage, his fingers squeezing my temples and tugging at my hair-roots. 'Then you can make some money and clear out of Pipalnagar. Delhi is the place to go! Why, I know a man who arrived in Delhi in 1947 with nothing but the clothes he wore and a few rupees. He began by selling thirsty travellers glasses of cold water at the railway station, then he opened a small tea shop; now he has two big restaurants and lives in a house as large as the prime minister's!'

Nobody intended to live in Pipalnagar forever. Delhi was the city most aspired to but as it was 200 miles away, few could afford to travel there.

Deep Chand would have shifted his trade to another town if he had had the capital. In Pipalnagar his main customers were small shopkeepers, factory workers and labourers from the railway station. 'Here I can charge only six annas for a haircut,' he lamented. 'In Delhi I could charge a rupee.'

IV

I was walking in the wheat fields beyond the railway tracks when I noticed a boy lying across the footpath, his head and shoulders hidden by wheat plants. I walked faster, and when I came near I saw that the boy's legs were twitching. He seemed to be having some kind of fit. The boy's face was white, his legs kept moving and his hands fluttered restlessly among the wheat stalks.

'What's the matter?' I said, kneeling down beside him but he was still unconscious.

I ran down the path to a Persian well, and dipping the end of my shirt in a shallow trough of water, soaked it well before returning to the boy. As I sponged his face the twitching ceased, and though he still breathed heavily, his face was calm and his hands still. He opened his eyes and stared at me, but he didn't really see me.

'You have bitten your tongue,' I said, wiping a little blood from the corner of his mouth. 'Don't worry. I'll stay here with you until you are all right.'

The boy raised himself and, resting his chin on his knees, he passed his arms around his drawn-up legs.

'I'm all right now,' he said.

'What happened?' I asked, sitting down beside him.

'Oh, it is nothing, it often happens. I don't know why. I cannot control it.'

'Have you been to a doctor?'

'Yes, when the fits first started, I went to the hospital. They gave me some pills that I had to take every day. But the pills made me so tired and sleepy that I couldn't work properly. So I stopped taking them. Now this happens once or twice a week. What does it matter? I'm all right when it's over and I do not feel anything when it happens.'

He got to his feet, dusting his clothes and smiling at me. He was a slim boy, long-limbed and bony. There was a little fluff on his cheeks and the promise of a moustache. He told me his name was Suraj, that he went to a night school in the city, and that he hoped to finish his high school exams in a few months' time. He was studying hard, he said, and if he passed he hoped to get a scholarship to a good college. If he failed, there was only the prospect of continuing in Pipalnagar.

I noticed a small tray of merchandise lying on the ground. It contained combs and buttons and little bottles of perfume. The tray was made to hang at Suraj's waist, supported by straps that went around his shoulders. All day he walked about Pipalnagar, sometimes covering ten or fifteen miles, selling odds and ends to people in their houses. He averaged about two rupees a day, which was enough for his food and other necessities; he managed to save about ten rupees a month for his school fees. He ate irregularly at little tea shops, at the stall near the bus stop, under the shady jamun and mango trees. When the jamun fruit was ripe, he would sit on a tree, sucking the sour fruit until his lips were stained purple. There was a small, nagging fear that he might get a fit while sitting on the tree and fall off, but the temptation to eat jamun was greater than his fear.

All this he told me while we walked through the fields towards the bazaar.

'Where do you live?' I asked. 'I'll walk home with you.'

'I don't live anywhere,' said Suraj. 'My home is not in Pipalnagar. Sometimes I sleep at the temple or at the railway station. In the summer months I sleep on the grass of the municipal park.'

'Well, wherever it is you stay, let me come with you.'

We walked together into the town, and parted near the bus stop. I returned to my room, and tried to do some writing while Suraj went to the bazaar to try selling his wares. We had agreed to meet each other again. I realized that Suraj was an epileptic, but there was nothing unusual about him being an orphan and a refugee. I liked his positive attitude to life. Most people in Pipalnagar were resigned to their circumstances but he was ambitious. I also liked his gentleness, his quiet voice, and the smile that flickered across his face regardless of whether he was sad or happy.

V

The temperature had touched forty-three degrees Celsius, and the small streets of Pipalnagar were empty. To walk barefoot on the scorching pavements was possible only for labourers, whose feet had developed several hard layers of protective skin; and now even these hardy men lay stretched out in the shade provided by trees and buildings.

I hadn't written anything in two weeks, and though one or two small payments were due from a Delhi newspaper, I could think of no substantial amount that was likely to come my way in the near future. I decided that I would dash off a couple of articles that same night, and post them the following morning.

Having made this comforting decision, I lay down on the floor in preference to the cot. I liked the touch of things; the touch of a cool floor on a hot day, the touch of earth—soft, grassy grass was good, especially dew-drenched grass. Wet earth was soft, sensuous, as was splashing through puddles and streams.

I slept, and dreamt of a cool, clear stream in a forest glade, where I bathed in gay abandon. A little further downstream was another bather. I hailed him, expecting to see Suraj but when the bather turned I found that it was my landlord's pot-bellied rent collector, holding an accounts ledger in his hands. This woke me up, and for the remainder of the day I worked feverishly at my articles.

Next morning, when I opened the door, I found Suraj asleep at the top of the steps. His tray lay at the bottom of the steps. He woke up as soon as I touched his shoulder.

'Have you been sleeping here all night?' I asked. 'Why didn't you come in?'

'It was very late,' said Suraj. 'I didn't want to disturb you.'

'Someone could have stolen your things while you were asleep.'

'Oh, I sleep quite lightly. Besides I have nothing of great value. But I came here to ask you a favour.'

'You need money?'

He laughed. 'Do all your friends mean money when they ask for favours? No, I want you to take your meal with me tonight.'

'But where? You have no place of your own and it would be too expensive in a restaurant.'

'In your room,' said Suraj. 'I shall bring the meat and vegetables and cook them here. Do you have a cooker?'

'I think so,' I said, scratching my head in some perplexity. 'I will have to look for it.'

Suraj brought a chicken for dinner—a luxury, one to be indulged in only two or three times a year. He had bought the bird for seven rupees, which was cheap. We spiced it and roasted it on a spit.

'I wish we could do this more often,' I said, as I dug my teeth into the soft flesh of a second chicken leg.

'We could do it at least once a month if we worked hard,' said Suraj.

'You know how to work. You work from morning to evening and then you work again.'

'But you are a writer. That is different. You have to wait for the right moment.'

I laughed. 'Moods and moments are for geniuses. No, it's really a matter of working hard, and I'm just plain lazy, to tell you the truth.'

'Perhaps you are writing the wrong things.'

'Perhaps, I wish I could do something else. Even if I repaired bicycle tyres, I'd make more money!'

'Then why don't you repair bicycle tyres?'

'Oh, I would rather be a bad writer than a good repairer of cycle tyres.' I brightened up, 'I could go into business, though. Do you know I once owned a vegetable stall?'

'Wonderful! When was that?'

'A couple of months ago. But it failed after two days.'

'Then you are not good at business. Let us think of something else.'

'I can tell fortunes with cards.'

'There are already too many fortune tellers in Pipalnagar.'

'Then we won't talk of fortunes. And you must sleep here tonight. It is better than sleeping on the roadside.'

VI

At noon when the shadows shifted and crossed the road, a band of children rushed down the empty street, shouting and waving their satchels. They had been at their desks from early morning, and now, despite the hot sun, they would have their fling while their elders slept on string charpoys beneath leafy neem trees.

On the soft sand near the riverbed, boys wrestled or played leapfrog. At alley corners, where tall buildings shaded narrow passages, the favourite game was gulli-danda. The gulli—a small piece of wood, about four inches long sharpened to a point at each end—is struck with the danda—a short, stout stick. A player is allowed three hits, and his score is the distance, in danda lengths, of his hits of the gulli. Boys who were experts at the game sent the gulli flying far down the road—sometimes into a shop or through a windowpane, which resulted in confusion, loud invective, and a dash for cover.

A game for both children and young men was kabaddi. This is a game that calls for good breath control and much agility. It is also known in different parts of India as hootoo-too, kho-kho and atya patya. Ramu, Deep Chand's younger brother, excelled at this game. He was the Pipalnagar kabaddi champion.

The game is played by two teams, consisting of eight or nine members each, who face each other across a dividing line. Each side in turn sends out one of its players into the opponent's area. This person has to keep on saying 'kabaddi, kabaddi' very fast and without taking a second breath. If he returns to his side after touching an opponent, that opponent is 'dead' and out of the game. If, however, he is caught and cannot struggle back to his side while still holding his breath, he is 'dead'.

Ramu, who was also a good wrestler, knew all the kabaddi holds, and was particularly good at capturing opponents. He had vitality and confidence, rare things in Pipalnagar. He wanted to go into the army after finishing school, a happy choice I thought.

VII

Suraj did not know if his parents were dead or alive. He had literally lost them when he was six. His father had been a farmer, a dark, unfathomable man who spoke little, thought perhaps even less and was vaguely aware he had a son—a weak boy given to introspection and dawdling at the riverbank when he should have been helping in the fields.

Suraj's mother had been a subdued, silent woman, frail and consumptive. Her husband seemed to expect that she would not live long, but Suraj did not know if she was living or dead. He had lost his parents at Amritsar railway station in the days of Partition, when trains coming across the border from Pakistan disgorged themselves of thousands of refugees or pulled into the station half-empty, drenched with blood and littered with corpses.

Suraj and his parents had been lucky to escape one of these massacres. Had they travelled on an earlier train (which they had tried desperately to catch), they might have been killed. Suraj was clinging to his mother's sari while she tried to keep up with her husband who was elbowing his way through the frightened, bewildered throng of refugees. Suraj collided with a burly Sikh and lost his grip on the sari. The Sikh had a long curved sword at his waist, and Suraj stared up at him in awe and fascination—at the man's long hair, which had fallen loose, at his wild black beard, and at the bloodstains on his white shirt. The Sikh pushed him aside and when Suraj looked around for his mother, she was not to be seen. She was hidden from him by a mass of restless bodies, all pushing in different directions. He could hear her calling his name and he tried to force his way through the crowd in the direction of her voice, but he was carried on the other way.

At night, when the platform emptied, he was still searching for his mother. Eventually, the police came and took him away. They looked for his parents but without success, and finally they sent him to a home for orphans. Many children lost their parents at about the same time.

Suraj stayed at the orphanage for two years and when he was eight, and felt himself a man, he ran away. He worked for some time as a helper in a tea shop; but when he started having epileptic fits the shopkeeper asked him to leave, and the boy found himself on the streets, begging for a living. He begged for a year, moving from one town to the next and finally ended up in Pipalnagar. By then he was twelve and really too old to beg, but he had saved some money, and with it he bought a small stock of combs, buttons, cheap perfumes and bangles, and, converting himself into a mobile shop, went from door to door selling his wares.

Pipalnagar is a small town and there was no house which Suraj hadn't visited. Everyone knew him; some had offered him food and drink; and the children liked him because he often played on a small flute when he went on his rounds.

VIII

Suraj came to see me quite often and, when he stayed late, he slept in my room, curling up on the floor and sleeping fitfully. He would always leave early in the morning before I could get him anything to eat.

'Should I go to Delhi, Suraj?' I asked him one evening.

'Why not? In Delhi, there are many ways of making money.'

'And spending it too. Why don't you come with me?'

'After my exams, perhaps. Not now.'

'Well, I can wait. I don't want to live alone in a big city.'

'In the meantime, write your book.'

'All right, I will try.'

We decided we could try to save a little money from Suraj's earnings and my own occasional payments from newspapers and magazines. Even if we were to give Delhi only a few days' trial, we would need money to live on. We managed to put away twenty rupees one week, but withdrew it the next when a friend, Pitamber, asked for a loan to repair his cycle rickshaw. He returned the money in three instalments but we could not save any of it. Pitamber and Deep Chand also had plans of going to Delhi. Pitamber wanted to own his own cycle rickshaw; Deep Chand dreamt of a swanky barber shop in the capital.

One day Suraj and I hired bicycles and rode out of Pipalnagar. It was a hot, sunny morning and we were perspiring after we had gone two miles, but a fresh wind sprang up suddenly, and we could smell the rain in the air though there were no clouds to be seen.

'Let us go where there are no people at all,' said Suraj. 'I am a little tired of people. I see too many of them all day.'

We got down from our cycles and, pushing them off the road, took a path through a paddy field and then one through a field of young maize, and in the distance we saw a tree, a crooked tree, growing beside a well. I do not even today know the name of that tree. I had never seen its kind before. It had a crooked trunk, crooked branches and it was clothed in thick, broad, crooked leaves, like the leaves on which food is served in bazaars.

In the trunk of the tree was a large hole and when I sat my cycle down with a crash, two green parrots flew out of the hole, and went dipping and swerving across the fields.

There was grass around the well, cropped short by grazing cattle, so we sat in the shade of the crooked tree and Suraj untied the red cloth in which we had brought food. We ate our bread and vegetable curry; meanwhile the parrots returned to the tree.

'Let us come here every week,' said Suraj, stretching himself out on the grass. It was a drowsy day, the air was humid and he soon fell asleep. I was aware of different sensations. I heard a cricket singing in the tree; the cooing of pigeons which lived in the walls of the old well; the soft breathing of Suraj; a rustling in the leaves of the tree; the distant drone of the bees. I smelt the grass and the old bricks around the well, and the promise of rain.

When I opened my eyes, I saw dark clouds on the horizon. Suraj was still sleeping with his arms thrown across his face to keep the glare out of his eyes. As I was thirsty, I went to the well and, putting my shoulders to it, turned the wheel very slowly, walking around the well four times, while cool clean water gushed out over the stones and along the channel to the fields. I drank from one of the trays, and the water tasted sweet; the deeper the wells, the sweeter the water. Suraj was sitting up now, looking at the sky.

'It's going to rain,' he said.

We pushed our cycles back to the main road and began riding homewards. We were a mile out of Pipalnagar when it began to rain. A lashing wind swept the rain across our faces, but we exulted in it and sang at the top of our voices until we reached the bus stop. Leaving the cycles at the hire shop, we ran up the rickety, swaying steps to my room.

In the evening, as the bazaar was lighting up, the rain stopped. We went to sleep quite early, but at midnight I was woken by the moon shining full on my face—a full moon, shedding its light all over Pipalnagar, peeping and prying into every home, washing the empty streets, silvering the corrugated tin roofs.

IX

The lizards hung listlessly on the walls and ceilings, waiting for the monsoon rains, which bring out all the insects from their cracks and crannies.

One day, clouds loomed upon the horizon, growing rapidly into enormous towers. A faint breeze sprang up, bringing with it the first of the monsoon raindrops. This was the moment everyone was waiting for. People ran out of their houses to take in the fresh breeze and the scent of those first few raindrops on the parched, dusty earth. Underground, in their cracks, the insects were moving. Termites and white ants, which had been sleeping through the hot season, emerged from their lairs.

And then, on the second or third night of the monsoon, came the great yearly flight of insects into the cool, brief freedom of the night. Out of every crack, from under the roots of trees, huge winged ants emerged, at first fluttering about heavily, on the first and last flight of their lives. At night there was only one direction in which they could fly—towards the light; towards the electric bulbs and smoky kerosene lamps throughout Pipalnagar. The street lamp opposite the bus stop, beneath my room, attracted a massive, quivering swarm of clumsy termites, which gave the impression of one thick, slowly-revolving body.

This was the hour of the lizards. Now they had their reward for those days of patient waiting. Plying their sticky pink tongues, they devoured the insects as fast as they came. For hours, they crammed their stomachs, knowing that such a feast would not be theirs again for another year. How wasteful nature is, I thought. Through the whole hot season the insect world prepares for the flight out of the darkness into light and not one of them survives its freedom.

Suraj and I walked barefooted over the cool, wet pavements, across the railway lines and the riverbed, until we were not far from the crooked tree. Dotting the landscape were old abandoned brick kilns. When it rained heavily, the hollows made by the kilns filled up with water. Suraj and I found a small tank where we could bathe and swim. On a mound in the middle of the tank stood a ruined hut, formerly inhabited by a watchman at the kiln. We swam and then wrestled on the young green grass. Though I was heavier than Suraj and my chest as sound as a new drum, he had a lot of power in his long, wiry arms and legs, and he pinioned me about the waist with his bony knees. And then suddenly, as I strained to press his back to the ground, I felt his body go tense. He stiffened, his thigh jerked against me and his legs began to twitch. I knew that a fit was coming on, but I was unable to get out of his grip. He held me more tightly as the fit took possession of him.

When I noticed his mouth working, I thrust the palm of my hand in, sideways, to prevent him from biting his tongue. But so violent was the convulsion that his teeth bit into my flesh. I shouted with pain and tried to pull my hand away, but he was unconscious and his jaw was set. I closed my eyes and counted slowly up to seven and then I felt his muscles relax and I was able to take my hand away. It was bleeding a little but I bound it with a handkerchief before Suraj fully regained consciousness.

He didn't say much as we walked back to town. He looked depressed and weak, but I knew it wouldn't take long for him to recover his usual good spirits. He did not notice that I kept my hand out of sight and only after he had returned from classes that night did he notice the bandage and asked what happened.

X

'Do you want to make some money?' asked Pitamber, bursting into the room like a festive cracker.

'I do,' I said.

'What do we have to do for it?' asked Suraj, striking a cautious note.

'Oh nothing, carry a banner and walk in front of a procession.'

'Why?'

'Don't ask me. Some political stunt.'

'Which party?'

'I don't know. Who cares? All I know is that they are paying two rupees a day to anyone who'll carry a flag or banner.'

'We don't need two rupees that badly,' I said. 'And you can make more than that in a day with your rickshaw.'

'True, but they're paying me *five*. They're fixing a loudspeaker to my rickshaw, and one of the party's men will sit in it and make speeches as we go along. Come on, it will be fun.'

'No banners for us,' I said. 'But we may come along and watch.'

And we did watch, when, later that morning, the procession passed along our street. It was a ragged procession of about a hundred people, shouting slogans. Some of them were children, and some of them were men who did not know what it was all about, but all joined in the slogan-shouting.

We didn't know much about it, either. Because, though the man in Pitamber's rickshaw was loud and eloquent, his loudspeaker was defective, with the result that his words were punctuated with squeaks and an eerie whining sound. Pitamber looked up and saw us standing on the balcony and gave us a wave and a wide grin. We decided to follow the procession at a discreet distance. It was a protest march against something or other; we never did manage to find out the details. The destination was the municipal office, and by the time we got there the crowd had increased to two or three hundred people. Some rowdies had now joined in, and things began to get out of hand. The man in the rickshaw continued his speech; another man standing on a wall was making a speech; and someone from the municipal office was confronting the crowd and making a speech of his own.

A stone was thrown, then another. From a sprinkling of stones, it soon became a shower of stones; and then some police constables, who had been standing by watching the fun, were ordered into action. They ran at the crowd where it was thinnest, brandishing stout sticks.

We were caught in the stampede that followed. A stone—flung no doubt at a policeman—was badly aimed and struck me on the shoulder. Suraj pulled me down a side street. Looking back, we saw Pitamber's cycle rickshaw lying on its side in the middle of the road, but there was no sign of Pitamber.

Later, he turned up in my room, with a cut over his left eyebrow which was bleeding freely. Suraj washed the cut, and I poured iodine over it—Pitamber did not flinch—and covered it with sticking plaster. The cut was quite deep and should have had stitches, but Pitamber was superstitious about hospitals, saying he knew very few people to come out of them alive. He was of course thinking about the Pipalnagar hospital.

So he acquired a scar on his forehead. It went rather well with his demonic good looks.

XI

'Thank God for the monsoon,' said Suraj. 'We won't have any more demonstrations on the roads until the weather improves!'

And, until the rain stopped, Pipalnagar was fresh and clean and alive. The children ran naked out of their houses and romped through the streets. The gutters overflowed, and the road became a mountain stream, coursing merrily towards the bus stop.

At the bus stop there was confusion. Newly arrived passengers, surrounded on all sides by a sea of mud and rainwater, were met by scores of tongas and cycle rickshaws, each jostling the other trying to cater to the passengers. As a result, only half found conveyances, while the other half found themselves knee-deep in Pipalnagar mud.

Pipalnagar mud has a quality all its own—and it is not easily removed or forgotten. Only buffaloes love it because it is soft and squelchy. Two parts of it are thick, sticky clay which seems to come alive at the slightest touch, clinging tenaciously to human flesh. Feet sink into it and have to be wrenched out. Fingers become webbed. Get it into your hair, and there is nothing you can do except go to Deep Chand and have your head shaved.

London has its fog, Paris its sewers, Pipalnagar its mud. Pitamber, of course, succeeded in getting as his passenger the most attractive girl to step off the bus, and showed her his skill and daring by taking her to her destination by the longest and roughest road.

The rain swirled over the trees and roofs of the town, and the parched earth soaked it up, giving out a fresh smell that came only once a year, the fragrance of quenched earth, that loveliest of all smells.

In my room I was battling against the elements, for the door would not close, and the rain swept into the room and soaked my cot. When finally I succeeded in closing the door, I discovered that the roof was leaking and the water was trickling down the walls, running through the dusty design I had made with my feet. I placed tins and mugs in strategic positions and, satisfied that everything was now under control, sat on the cot to watch the rooftops through my windows.

There was a loud banging on the door. It flew open, and there was Suraj standing on the threshold, drenched. Coming in, he began to dry himself while I made desperate efforts to close the door again.

'Let's make some tea,' he said.

Glasses of hot, sweet milky tea on a rainy day…it was enough to make me feel fresh and full of optimism. We sat on the cot, enjoying the brew.

'One day, I'll write a book,' I said. 'Not just a thriller, but a real book, about real people. Perhaps about you and me and Pipalnagar. And then we'll be famous and our troubles will be over and new troubles will begin. I don't mind problems as long as they are new. While you're studying, I'll write my book. I'll start tonight. It is an auspicious time, the first night of the monsoon.'

A tree must have fallen across the wires somewhere, because the lights would not come on. So I lit a small oil lamp, and while it spluttered in the steamy darkness Suraj opened his book and, with one hand on the book, the other playing with his toe—this helped him to concentrate!—he began to study. I took the inkpot down from the shelf, and finding it empty, added a little rainwater to it from one of the mugs. I sat down beside Suraj and began to write, but the pen was no good and made blotches all over the paper. And, although I was full of writing just then, I didn't really know what I wanted to say.

So I went out and began pacing up and down the road. There I found Pitamber, a little drunk, very merry, and prancing about in the middle of the road.

'What are you dancing for?' I asked.

'I'm happy, so I'm dancing,' said Pitamber.

'And why are you happy?' I asked.

'Because I'm dancing,' he said.

The rain stopped and the neem trees gave out a strong, sweet smell.

XII

Flowers in Pipalnagar—did they exist? As a child I knew a garden in Lucknow where there were beds of phlox and petunias and another garden where only roses grew. In the fields around Pipalnagar was thorn apple—a yellow buttercup nestling among thorn leaves. But in Pipalnagar Bazaar there were no flowers except one—a marigold growing out of a crack on my balcony. I had removed the plaster from the base of the plant, and filled in a little earth which I watered every morning. The plant was healthy, and sometimes it produced a small orange marigold.

Sometimes Suraj plucked a flower and kept it in his tray, among the combs, buttons and scent bottles. Sometimes he gave the flower to a passing child, once to a small boy who immediately tore it to shreds. Suraj was back on his rounds, as his exams were over.

Whenever he was tired of going from house to house, Suraj would sit beneath a shady banyan or peepul tree, put his tray aside, and take out his flute. The haunting notes travelled down the road in the afternoon stillness, drawing children to him. They would sit beside him and be very quiet when he played, because there was something melancholic and appealing about the tune. Suraj sometimes made flutes out of pieces of bamboo, but he never sold them. He would give them to the children he liked. He would sell almost anything, but not flutes.

Suraj sometimes played the flute at night, when he lay awake, unable to sleep; but even though I slept, I could hear the music in my dreams. Sometimes he took his flute with him to the crooked tree and played for the benefit of the birds. The parrots made harsh noises in response and flew away. Once, when Suraj was playing his flute to a small group of children, he had a fit. The flute fell from his hands. And he began to roll about in the dust on the roadside. The children became frightened and ran away, but they did not stay away for long. The next time they heard the flute, they came to listen as usual.

XIII

It was Lord Krishna's birthday, and the rain came down as heavily as it is said to have done on the day he was born. Krishna is the best beloved of all the gods. Young mothers laugh or weep as they read or hear the pranks of his boyhood; young men pray to be as tall and as strong as Krishna was when he killed King Kamsa's elephant and wrestlers; young girls dream of a lover as daring as Krishna to carry them off in a war chariot; grown men envy the wisdom and statesmanship with which he managed the affairs of his kingdom.

The rain came so unexpectedly that it took everyone by surprise. In seconds, people were drenched, and within minutes, the streets were flooded. The temple tank overflowed, the railway lines disappeared, and the old wall near the bus stop shivered and silently fell—the sound of its collapse drowned in the downpour. A naked young man with a dancing bear cavorted in the middle of the vegetable market. Pitamber's rickshaw churned through the floodwater while he sang lustily as he worked.

Wading through knee-deep water down the road, I saw the roadside vendors salvaging whatever they could. Plastic toys, cabbages and utensils floated away and were seized by urchins. The water had risen to the level of the shop fronts and the floors were awash. Deep Chand and Ramu, with the help of a customer, were using buckets to bail the water out of their shop. The rain stopped as suddenly as it had begun and the sun came out. The water began to find an outlet, flooding other low-lying areas, and a paper boat came sailing between my legs.

Next morning, the morning on which the result of Suraj's examinations was due, I rose early—the first time I ever got up before Suraj—and went down to the news agency. A small crowd of students had gathered at the bus stop, joking with each other and hiding their nervousness with a show of indifference. There were not many passengers on the first bus, and there was a mad grab for newspapers as the bundle landed with a thud on the pavement. Within half-an-hour, the newsboy had sold all his copies. It was the best day of the year for him.

I went through the columns relating to Pipalnagar, but I couldn't find Suraj's roll number on the list of successful candidates. I had the number on a slip of paper, and I looked at it again to make sure I had compared it correctly with the others; then I went through the newspaper once more. When I returned to the room, Suraj was sitting on the doorstep. I didn't have to tell him he had failed—he knew by the look on my face. I sat down beside him, and we said nothing for some time.

'Never mind,' Suraj said eventually. 'I will pass next time.'

I realized I was more depressed than he was and that he was trying to console me.

'If only you'd had more time,' I said.

'I have a year. And you will have time to finish your book, and then we can go away together. Another year of Pipalnagar won't be so bad. As long as I have your friendship almost everything can be tolerated.'

He stood up, the tray hanging from his shoulders. 'Is there anything you'd like to buy?'

XIV

Another year of Pipalnagar! But it was not to be. A short time later, I received a letter from the editor of a newspaper, calling me to Delhi for an interview. My friends insisted that I should go. Such an opportunity would not come again.

But I needed a shirt. The few I possessed were either frayed at the collar or torn at the shoulders. I hadn't been able to afford a new shirt for over a year, and I couldn't afford one now. Struggling writers weren't expected to dress well, but I felt in order to get the job I would need both a haircut and a clean shirt.

Where was I to go to get a shirt? Suraj generally wore an old red-striped T-shirt; he washed it every second evening, and by morning it was dry and ready to wear again; but it was tight even on him. He did not have another. Besides, I needed something white, something respectable!

I went to Deep Chand who had a collection of shirts. He was only too glad to lend me one. But they were all brightly coloured—pinks, purples and magentas... No editor was going to be impressed by a young writer in a pink shirt. They looked fine on Deep Chand, but he had no need to look respectable.

Finally, Pitamber came to my rescue. He didn't bother with shirts himself, except in winter, but he was able to borrow a clean white shirt from a guard at the jail, who'd got it from the relative of a convict in exchange for certain favours.

'This shirt will make you look respectable,' said Pitamber. 'To be respectable—what an adventure!'

XV

Freedom. The moment the bus was out of Pipalnagar, and the fields opened out on all sides, I knew that I was free, that I had always been free. Only my own weakness, hesitation, and the habits that had grown around me had held me back. All I had to do was sit in a bus and go somewhere.

I sat near the open window of the bus and let the cool breeze from the fields play against my face. Herons and snipe waded among the lotus roots in flat green ponds. Blue jays swooped around telegraph poles. Children jumped naked into the canals that wound through the fields. Because I was happy, it seemed to me that everyone else was happy—the driver, the conductor, the passengers, the farmers in the fields and those driving bullock carts. When two women behind me started quarrelling over their seats, I helped to placate them. Then I took a small girl on my knee and pointed out camels, buffaloes, vultures and pariah dogs.

Six hours later, the bus crossed the bridge over the swollen Yamuna River, passed under the walls of the great Red Fort built by a Mughal emperor, and entered the old city of Delhi. I found it strange to be in a city again, after several years in Pipalnagar. It was a little frightening too. I felt like a stranger. No one was interested in me.

In Pipalnagar, people wanted to know each other, or at least to know about one another. In Delhi, no one cared who you were or where you came from, like big cities almost everywhere. It was prosperous but without a heart.

After a day and a night of loneliness, I found myself wishing that Suraj had accompanied me; wishing that I was back in Pipalnagar. But when the job was offered to me—at a starting salary of three hundred rupees per month, a princely sum compared to what I had been making on my own—I did not have the courage to refuse it. After accepting the job—which was to commence in a week's time—I spent the day wandering through the bazaars, down the wide, shady roads of the capital, resting under the jamun trees, and thinking all the time what I would do in the months to come.

I slept at the railway waiting room and all night long I heard the shunting and whistling of engines which conjured up visions of places with sweet names like Kumbakonam, Krishnagiri, Polonnarurawa. I dreamt of palm-fringed beaches and inland lagoons; of the echoing chambers of deserted cities, red sandstone and white marble; of temples in the sun; and elephants crossing wide, slow-moving rivers...

XVI

Pitamber was on the platform when the train steamed into

the Pipalnagar station in the early hours of a damp September morning. I waved to him from the carriage window, and shouted that everything had gone well.

But everything was not well here. When I got off the train, Pitamber told me that Suraj had been ill—that he'd had a fit on a lonely stretch of road the previous afternoon and had lain in the sun for over an hour. Pitamber had found him, suffering from heatstroke, and brought him home. When I saw him, he was sitting up on the string bed drinking hot tea. He looked pale and weak, but his smile was reassuring.

'Don't worry,' he said. 'I will be all right.'

'He was bad last night,' said Pitamber. 'He had a fever and kept talking, as in a dream. But what he says is true—he is better this morning.'

'Thanks to Pitamber,' said Suraj. 'It is good to have friends.'

'Come with me to Delhi, Suraj,' I said. 'I have got a job now. You can live with me and attend a school regularly.'

'It is good for friends to help each other,' said Suraj, 'but only after I have passed my exam will I join you in Delhi. I made myself this promise. Poor Pipalnagar—nobody wants to stay here. Will you be sorry to leave?'

'Yes, I will be sorry. A part of me will still be here.'

XVII

Deep Chand was happy to know that I was leaving. 'I'll follow you soon,' he said. 'There is money to be made in Delhi, cutting hair. Girls are keeping it short these days.'

'But men are growing it long.'

'True. So I shall open a barber shop for ladies and a beauty salon for men! Ramu can attend to the ladies.'

Ramu winked at me in the mirror. He was still at the stage of teasing girls on their way to school or college.

The snip of Deep Chand's scissors made me sleepy, as I sat in his chair. His fingers beat a rhythmic tattoo on my scalp.

It was my last haircut in Pipalnagar, and Deep Chand did not charge me for it. I promised to write as soon as I had settled down in Delhi.

The next day when Suraj was stronger, I said, 'Come, let us go for a walk and visit our crooked tree. Where is your flute, Suraj?'

'I don't know. Let us look for it.'

We searched the room and our belongings for the flute but could not find it.

'It must have been left on the roadside,' said Suraj. 'Never mind. I will make another.'

I could picture the flute lying in the dust on the roadside and somehow this made me sad. But Suraj was full of high spirits as we walked across the railway lines and through the fields.

'The rains are over,' he said, kicking off his chappals and lying down on the grass. 'You can smell the autumn in the air. Somehow, it makes me feel light-hearted. Yesterday I was sad, and tomorrow I might be sad again, but today I know that I am happy. I want to live on and on. One lifetime cannot satisfy my heart.'

'A day in a lifetime,' I said. 'I'll remember this day—the way the sun touches us, the way the grass bends, the smell of this leaf as I crush it...'

XVIII

Every morning at six the first bus arrives, and the passengers alight, looking sleepy and dishevelled and rather discouraged by their first sight of Pipalnagar. When they have gone their various ways, the bus is driven into the shed. Cows congregate at the dustbin and the pavement dwellers come to life, stretching their tired limbs on the hard stone steps. I carry the bucket up the steps to my room, and bathe for the last time on the open balcony. In the villages, the buffaloes are wallowing in green ponds while naked urchins sit astride them, scrubbing their backs, and a crow or water bird perches on their glistening necks. The parrots are busy in the crooked tree, and a slim green snake basks in the sun on our island near the brick kiln. In the hills, the mists have lifted and the distant mountains are fringed with snow.

It is autumn, and the rains are over. The earth meets the sky in one broad, bold sweep.

A land of thrusting hills. Terraced hills, wood-covered and windswept. Mountains where the gods speak gently to the lonely. Hills of green grass and grey rock, misty at dawn, hazy at noon, molten at sunset, where fierce, fresh torrents rush to the valleys below. A quiet land of fields and ponds, shaded by ancient trees and ringed with palms, where sacred rivers are touched by temples, where temples are touched by southern seas.

This is the land I should write about. Pipalnagar should be forgotten. I should turn aside from it to sing instead of the splendours of exotic places.

But only yesterdays are truly splendid... And there are other singers, sweeter than I, to sing of tomorrow. I can only write of today, of Pipalnagar, where I have lived and loved.

THE FUNERAL

'I don't think he should go,' said Aunt M.

'He's too young,' concurred Aunt B. 'He'll get upset and probably throw a tantrum. And you know Padre Lal doesn't like having children at funerals.'

The boy said nothing. He sat in the darkest corner of the darkened room, his face revealing nothing of what he thought and felt. His father's coffin lay in the next room, the lid fastened forever over the tired, wistful countenance of the man who had meant so much to the boy. Nobody else had mattered—neither uncles nor aunts nor fond grandparents. Least of all the mother who was hundreds of miles away with another husband. He hadn't seen her since he was four—that was just over five years ago—and he did not remember her very well.

The house was full of people—friends, relatives, neighbours. Some had tried to fuss over him but had been discouraged by his silence, the absence of tears. The more understanding of them had kept their distance.

Scattered words of condolence passed back and forth like dragonflies in the wind. 'Such a tragedy!'

'Only forty.'

'No one realized how serious it was.'

'Devoted to the child.'

It seemed to the boy that everyone who mattered in the hill station was present. And for the first time they had the run of the house for his father had not been a sociable man. Books, music, flowers and his stamp collection had been his main preoccupations, apart from the boy.

A small hearse, drawn by a hill pony, was led in at the gate and several able-bodied men lifted the coffin and manoeuvred it into the carriage. The crowd drifted away. The cemetery was about a mile down the road and those who did not have cars would have to walk the distance.

The boy stared through a window at the small procession passing through the gate. He'd been forgotten for the moment— left in care of the servants, who were the only ones to stay behind. Outside it was misty. The mist had crept up the valley and settled like a damp towel on the face of the mountain. Everyone was wet although it hadn't rained.

The boy waited until everyone had gone and then he left the room and went out onto the veranda. The gardener, who had been sitting in a bed of nasturtiums, looked up and asked the boy if he needed anything. But the boy shook his head and retreated indoors. The gardener, looking aggrieved because of the damage done to the flower beds by the mourners, shambled off to his quarters. The sahib's death meant that he would be out of a job very soon. The house would pass into other hands. The boy would go to an orphanage. There weren't many people who kept gardeners these days. In the kitchen, the cook was busy preparing the only big meal ever served in the house. All those relatives, and the padre too, would come back famished, ready for a sombre but nevertheless substantial meal. He, too, would be out of a job soon; but cooks were always in demand.

The boy slipped out of the house by a back door and made his way into the lane through a gap in a thicket of dog roses. When he reached the main road, he could see the mourners wending their way around the hill to the cemetery. He followed at a distance.

It was the same road he had often taken with his father during their evening walks. The boy knew the name of almost every plant and wildflower that grew on the hillside. These, and various birds and insects, had been described and pointed out to him by his father.

Looking northwards, he could see the higher ranges of the Himalayas and the eternal snows. The graves in the cemetery were so laid out that if their incumbents did happen to rise one day, the first thing they would see would be the glint of the sun on those snow-covered peaks. Possibly the site had been chosen for the view. But to the boy it did not seem as if anyone would be able to thrust aside those massive tombstones and rise from their graves to enjoy the view. Their rest seemed as eternal as the snows. It would take an earthquake to burst those stones asunder and thrust the coffins up from the earth. The boy wondered why people hadn't made it easier for the dead to rise. They were so securely entombed that it appeared as though no one really wanted them to get out.

'God has need of your father...' With those words a well-meaning missionary had tried to console him.

And had God, in the same way, laid claim to the thousands of men, women and children who had been put to rest here in these neat and serried rows? What could he have wanted them for? Of what use are we to God when we are dead, wondered the boy.

The cemetery gate stood open but the boy leant against the old stone wall and stared down at the mourners as they shuffled about with the unease of a batsman about to face a very fast bowler. Only this bowler was invisible and would come up stealthily and from behind.

Padre Lal's voice droned on through the funeral service and then the coffin was lowered—down, deep down. The boy was surprised at how far down it seemed to go! Was that other, better world down in the depths of the earth? How could anyone, even a Samson, push his way back to the surface again? Superman did it in comics but his father was a gentle soul who wouldn't fight too hard against the earth and the grass and the roots of tiny trees. Or perhaps he'd grow into a tree and escape that way! 'If ever I'm put away like this,' thought the boy, 'I'll get into the root of a plant and then I'll become a flower and then maybe a bird will come and carry my seed away... I'll get out somehow!'

A few more words from the padre and then some of those present threw handfuls of earth over the coffin before moving away.

Slowly, in twos and threes, the mourners departed. The mist swallowed them up. They did not see the boy behind the wall. They were getting hungry.

He stood there until they had all gone. Then he noticed that the gardeners or caretakers were filling in the grave. He did not know whether to go forward or not. He was a little afraid. And it was too late now. The grave was almost covered.

He turned and walked away from the cemetery. The road stretched ahead of him, empty, swathed in mist. He was alone. What had his father said to him once? 'The strongest man in the world is he who stands alone.'

Well, he was alone, but at the moment he did not feel very strong.

For a moment he thought his father was beside him, that they were together on one of their long walks. Instinctively he put out his hand, expecting his father's warm, comforting touch. But there was nothing there, nothing, no one...

He clenched his fists and pushed them deep down into his pockets. He lowered his head so that no one would see his tears. There were people in the mist but he did not want to go near them for they had put his father away.

'He'll find a way out,' the boy said fiercely to himself. 'He'll get out somehow!'

SOME HILL STATION GHOSTS

Simla has its phantom rickshaw and Lansdowne its headless horseman. Mussoorie has its woman in white. Late at night, she can be seen sitting on the parapet wall on the winding road up to the hill station. Don't stop to offer her a lift. She will fix you with her evil eye and ruin your holiday.

The Mussoorie taxi drivers and other locals call her Bhoot Aunty. Everyone has seen her at some time or the other. To give her a lift is to court disaster. Many accidents have been attributed to her baleful presence. And when people pick themselves up from the road (or are picked up by concerned citizens), Bhoot Aunty is nowhere to be seen, although survivors swear that she was in the car with them.

Ganesh Saili, Abha and I were coming back from Dehradun late one night when we saw this woman in white sitting on the parapet by the side of the road. As our headlights fell on her, she turned her face away; Ganesh, being a thorough gentleman, slowed down and offered her a lift. She turned towards us, and smiled a wicked smile. She seemed quite attractive except that her canines protruded slightly in vampire fashion.

'Don't stop!' screamed Abha. 'Don't even look at her! It's Aunty!'

Ganesh pressed down on the accelerator and sped past her. Next day we heard that a tourist's car had gone off the road and the occupants had been severely injured. The accident took place shortly after they had stopped to pick up a woman in white who had wanted a lift. But she was not among the injured.

Miss Ripley-Bean, an old English lady who was my neighbour when I lived near Wynberg-Allen School, told me that her family was haunted by a malignant phantom head that always appeared before the death of one of her relatives.

She said her brother saw this apparition the night before her mother died, and both she and her sister saw it before the death of their father. The sister slept in the same room. They were both awakened one night by a curious noise in the cupboard facing their beds. One of them got out of bed to see if their cat was in the room, when the cupboard door suddenly opened and a luminous head appeared. It was covered with matted hair and appeared to be in an advanced stage of decomposition. Its fleshless mouth grinned at the terrified sisters. And then as they crossed themselves, it vanished. The next day they learned that their father, who was in Lucknow, had died suddenly, at about the time that they had seen the dead head.

Everyone likes to hear stories about haunted houses; even sceptics will listen to a ghost story, while casting doubts on its veracity.

Rudyard Kipling wrote a number of memorable ghost stories set in India—'The Return of Imray', 'The Phantom Rickshaw', 'The Mark of the Beast', 'At the End of the Passage'—his favourite milieu being the haunted dak bungalow. But it was only after his return to England that he found himself actually having to live in a haunted house. He writes about it in his autobiography, *Something of Myself.*

> The spring of '96 saw us in Torquay, where we found a house for our heads that seemed almost too good to be true. It was large and bright, with big rooms each and all open to the sun, the ground embellished with great trees and the warm land dipping southerly to the clean sea under

the Mary Church cliffs. It had been inhabited for thirty years by three old maids.

The revelation came in the shape of a growing depression which enveloped us both—a gathering blackness of mind and sorrow of the heart, that each put down to the new, soft climate and, without telling the other, fought against for long weeks. It was the feng shui—the Spirit of the house itself—that darkened the sunshine and fell upon us every time we entered, checking the very words on our lips... We paid forfeit and fled. More than thirty years later we returned down the steep little road to that house, and found, quite unchanged, the same brooding spirit of deep despondency within the rooms.

Again, thirty years later, he returned to this house in his short story, 'The House Surgeon', in which two sisters cannot come to terms with the suicide of a third sister, and brood upon the tragedy day and night until their thoughts saturate every room of the house.

Many years ago, I had a similar experience in a house in Dehradun, in which an elderly English couple had died from neglect and starvation. In 1947, when many European residents were leaving the town and emigrating to the UK, this poverty-stricken old couple, sick and friendless, had been forgotten. Too ill to go out for food or medicine, they had died in their beds, where they were discovered several days later by the landlord's munshi.

The house stood empty for several years. No one wanted to live in it. As a young man, I would sometimes roam about the neglected grounds or explore the cold, bare rooms, now stripped of furniture, doorless and windowless, and I would be assailed by a feeling of deep gloom and depression. Of course, I knew what had happened there, and that may have contributed to the effect the place had on me. But when I took a friend, Jai

Shankar, through the house, he told me he felt quite sick with apprehension and fear. 'Ruskin, why have you brought me to this awful house?' he said. 'I'm sure it's haunted.' And only then did I tell him about the tragedy that had taken place within its walls.

Today, the house is used as a government office. No one lives in it at night except for a Gurkha chowkidar, a man of strong nerves who sleeps on the back veranda. The atmosphere of the place doesn't bother him, but he does hear strange sounds in the night. 'Like someone crawling about on the floor above,' he tells me. 'And someone groaning. These old houses are noisy places...'

A morgue is not a noisy place, as a rule. And for a morgue attendant, corpses are silent companions.

Old Mr Jacob, who lives just behind the cottage, was once a morgue attendant for the local mission hospital. In those days it was situated at Sunny Bank, about a hundred metres up the hill from here. One of the outhouses served as the morgue: Mr Jacob begs me not to identify it.

He tells me of a terrifying experience he went through when he was doing night duty at the morgue.

'The body of a young man was found floating in the Aglar River, behind Landour, and was brought to the morgue while I was on night duty. It was placed on the table and covered with a sheet.

'I was quite accustomed to seeing corpses of various kinds and did not mind sharing the same room with them, even after dark. On this occasion a friend had promised to join me, and to pass the time I strolled around the room, whistling a popular tune. I think it was "Danny Boy", if I remember right. My friend was a long time coming, and I soon got tired of whistling and sat down on the bench beside the table. The night was very still, and I began to feel uneasy. My thoughts went to the boy who had drowned and I wondered what he had been like when he was alive. Dead bodies are so impersonal...

'The morgue had no electricity, just a kerosene lamp, and after some time I noticed that the flame was very low. As I was about to turn it up, suddenly it went out. I lit the lamp again, after extending the wick. I returned to the bench, but I had not been sitting there for long when the lamp again went out, and something moved very softly and quietly past me.

'I felt quite sick and faint, and could hear my heart pounding away. The strength had gone out of my legs, otherwise I would have fled from the room. I felt weak and helpless, unable even to call out.

'Presently the footsteps came nearer and nearer. Something cold and icy touched one of my hands and felt its way up towards my neck and throat. It was behind me, then it was before me. Then it was *over* me. I was in the arms of the corpse!

'I must have fainted, because when I woke up I was on the floor, and my friend was trying to revive me. The corpse was back on the table.'

'It may have been a nightmare,' I suggested. 'Or you allowed your imagination to run riot.'

'No,' said Mr Jacobs. 'There were wet, slimy marks on my clothes. And the feet of the corpse matched the wet footprints on the floor.'

After this experience, Mr Jacobs refused to do any more night duty at the morgue.

From Herbertpur near Paonta Sahib you can go up to Kalsi, and then up the hill road to Chakrata.

Chakrata is in a security zone, most of it off limits to tourists, which is one reason why it has remained unchanged in 150 years of its existence. Today, the population of this small town is 1,500 which was the same in 1947. It is probably the only town in India that hasn't shown a population increase.

I was fortunate enough to be able to stay in the forest rest house on the outskirts of the town, courtesy a government official. This is a new building, the old rest house—a little way downhill—having fallen into disuse. The chowkidar told me the old rest house was haunted, and that this was the real reason for its having been abandoned. I was a bit sceptical about this, and asked him what kind of haunting took place in it. He told me that he had himself gone through a frightening experience in the old house, when he had gone there to light a fire for some forest officers who were expected that night. After lighting the fire, he looked round and saw a large black animal, like a wild cat, sitting on the wooden floor and gazing into the fire. 'I called out to it, thinking it was someone's pet. The creature turned, and looked full at me with eyes that were human, and a face which was the face of an ugly woman. The creature snarled at me, and the snarl became an angry howl. And then it vanished!'

'And what did you do?' I asked.

'I vanished too,' said the chowkidar. 'I haven't been down to that house again.'

I did not volunteer to sleep in the old house but made myself comfortable in the new one, where I hoped I would not be troubled by any phantom. However, a large rat kept me company, gnawing away at the woodwork of a chest of drawers. Whenever I switched on the light it would be silent, but as soon as the light was off, it would start gnawing away again.

This reminded me of a story old Miss Kellner (of my Dehra childhood) told me, of a young man who was desperately in love with a girl who did not care for him. One day, when he was following her in the street, she turned on him and, pointing to a rat which some boys had just killed, said, 'I'd as soon marry that rat as marry you.' He took her cruel words so much to heart that he pined away and died. After his death the girl was haunted at night by a rat and occasionally she would be bitten. When the family decided to emigrate, they travelled down to

Bombay in order to embark on a ship sailing for London. The ship had just left the quay, when shouts and screams were heard from the pier. The crowd scattered, and a huge rat with fiery eyes ran down to the end of the quay. It sat there, screaming with rage, then jumped into the water and disappeared. After that (according to Miss Kellner), the girl was not haunted again.

Old dak bungalows and forest rest houses have a reputation for being haunted. And most hill stations have their resident ghosts—and ghost writers! But I will not extend this catalogue of ghostly hauntings and visitations, as I do not want to discourage tourists from visiting Landour and Mussoorie. In some countries, ghosts are an added attraction for tourists. Britain boasts hundreds of haunted castles and stately homes, and visitors to Romania seek out Transylvania and Dracula's Castle. So, do we promote Bhoot Aunty as a tourist attraction? Only if she reforms and stops sending vehicles off those hairpin bends that lead to Mussoorie.

A HILL STATION'S VINTAGE MURDERS

There is less crime in the hills than in the plains, and so the few murders that do take place from time to time stand out as landmarks in the annals of a hill station.

Among the gravestones in the Mussoorie Cemetery there is one which bears the inscription: 'Murdered by the hand he befriended.' This is the grave of Mr James Reginald Clapp, a chemist's assistant, who was brutally done to death on the night of 31 August 1909.

Miss Ripley-Bean, who has spent most of her eighty-seven years in this hill station, remembers the case clearly, though she was only a girl at the time. From the details she has given me, and from a brief account in *A Mussoorie Miscellany*, now out of print, I am able to reconstruct this interesting case and a couple of others which were the sensations of their respective 'seasons'.

Mr Clapp was an assistant in the chemist's shop of Messrs J. B. & E. Samuel (no longer in existence), situated in one of the busiest sections of the Mall. At that time the adjoining cantonment of Landour was an important convalescent centre for British soldiers. Mr Clapp was popular with the soldiers, and he had befriended some of them when they had run short of money. He was a steady worker and sent most of his savings home, to his mother in Birmingham; she was planning to use the money to buy the house in which she lived.

At the time of the murder, Clapp was particularly friendly with a Corporal Allen, who was eventually to be hanged at the Naini Jail. The murder was brutal, the initial attack being launched with a soda-water bottle on the victim's head. Clapp's throat was then cut from ear to ear with his own razor, which was left behind in the room. The body was discovered on the floor of the shop the next morning by the proprietor, Mr Samuel, who did not live on the premises.

Suspicion immediately fell on Corporal Allen because he had left Mussoorie that same night, arriving at Rajpur in the foothills (a seven-mile walk by the bridle path) many hours later than he was expected at a Rajpur boarding house. According to some, Clapp had last been seen in the corporal's company.

There was other circumstantial evidence pointing to Allen's guilt. On the day of the murder, Mr Clapp had received his salary, and this sum, in sovereigns and notes, was never traced. Allen was alleged to have made a payment in sovereigns at Rajpur. Someone had given Allen a biscuit tin packed with sandwiches for his journey down, and it was thought that perhaps the tin had been used by the murderer as a safe for the money. But no tin was found, and Allen denied having had one with him.

Allen was arrested at Rajpur and brought back to Mussoorie under escort. He was taken immediately to the victim's bedside, where the body still lay, the police hoping that he might confess his guilt when confronted with the body of the victim; but Allen was unmoved, and protested his innocence.

Meanwhile, other soldiers from among Mr Clapp's friends had gathered on the Mall. They had removed their belts and were ready to lynch Allen as soon as he was brought out of the shop. The situation was tense, but further mishap was averted by the resourcefulness of Mr Rust, a photographer, who, being of the same build as the corporal, put on an army coat with a turned-up collar, and arranged to be handcuffed between two policemen. He remained with them inside the shop, in partial view of the mob, while the rest of the police party escorted the corporal out by a back entrance. Mr Rust did not abandon his disguise or leave the shop until word arrived that Allen was secure in the police station.

Corporal Allen was eventually found guilty, and was hanged. But there were many who felt that he had never really been proved guilty, and that he had been convicted on purely circumstantial evidence; and looking back on the case from this distance in time one cannot help feeling that the soldier may have been a victim of circumstances, and perhaps of local prejudice, for he was not liked by his fellows. Allen himself hinted that he was not in the vicinity of the crime that night but in the company of a lady whose integrity he was determined to shield. If this was true, it was a pity that the lady prized her virtue more than her friend's life, for she did not come forward to save him. The chaplain who administered to Allen during his last days in the 'condemned cell' was prepared to absolve the corporal and could not accept that he was a murderer.

One of the hill station's most sensational crimes was committed on 25 July 1927, at the height of the 'season', and in the heart of the town, in Zephyr Hall, then a boarding house. It provided a good deal of excitement for the residents of the boarding house.

Soon after midday, Zephyr Hall residents were startled into brisk activity when a woman screamed and a shot rang out from one of the rooms. Other shots followed in rapid succession.

Those boarders who happened to be in the public lounge or veranda dived for the safety of their rooms; but one unhappy resident, taking the precaution of coming around a corner with his hands held well above his head, ran straight into a levelled pistol. And the man with the gun, who had just killed his wife and wounded his daughter, was still able to see some humour in the situation, for he burst into laughter! The boarder escaped unhurt. But the murderer, Mr Owen, did not savour the situation for long. He shot himself long before the police arrived.

The final crime I'd like to write about is the most convoluted of the three, which is probably why it drew the attention of the world's greatest crime writers. Arthur Conan Doyle, the creator of Sherlock Holmes, had a lifelong interest in unusual criminal cases, and his friends often passed on to him interesting accounts of crime and detection from around the world. It was in this way that he learnt of the strange death of Miss Frances Garnett-Orme in Mussoorie. Here was a murder combining the weird borders of the occult with a crime mystery as inexplicable as any devised by Doyle himself.

In April 1912 (shortly before the *Titanic* went down) Conan Doyle received a letter from his Sussex neighbour Rudyard Kipling:

Dear Doyle,

There has been a murder in India... A murder by suggestion at Mussoorie, which is one of the most curious things in its line of record.

Everything that is improbable, and on the face of it impossible, is in this case.

Kipling received details of the case from a friend working at the Allahabad *Pioneer*, a paper for which, as a young man, he had worked in the 1880s. Urging Doyle to pursue the story Kipling concluded: 'The psychology alone is beyond description.'

Doyle was interested to hear more, for India had furnished him with material in the past, as in *The Sign of the Four* and several short stories. Kipling, too, had turned to crime and detection in his early stories of Strickland, the Anglo-Indian policeman. The two writers got together and discussed the case, which was indeed a fascinating affair. (The extracts from their correspondence were sent to me by Peter Costello, a biographer of Doyle.)

It was during the summer 'season' of 1911 that Miss Frances

Garnett-Orme came to stay in Mussoorie, taking a suite at the Savoy, a popular resort hotel. On 28 July she celebrated her forty-ninth birthday. She was the daughter of George Garnett-Orme, a district registrar of the country court of Skipton-in-Craven in Yorkshire. Her family was important enough to be counted among the landed gentry. George Garnett-Orme had died in 1892.

Miss Frances Garnett-Orme came to India in 1893 with the intention of marrying Jack Grant of the United Provinces Police. But he died in 1894 and she went back to England. Upset by his death following so soon after her father's, she turned to spiritualism in the hope of communicating with him. We must remember that spiritualism was all the rage in the early years of the century. Seances and table-rapping was part of the social scene both in England and India. Madame Blavatsky, the chief exponent of spiritualism, was probably at the height of her popularity around this time—she spent her 'seasons' in neighbouring Simla, where she had many followers.

Miss Garnet-Orme's life was unsettled. She was drawn back to India, returning in 1901 to live in Lucknow, the regional capital of the United Provinces. She was still in contact with Jack Grant's family and saw his brother occasionally. The summer of 1907 was spent at Nainital, a hill station popular with Lucknow residents. It was here that she met Miss Eva Mountstephen, who was working as a governess.

Eva Mountstephen, too, had an interest in spiritualism. It appears that she had actually told several of her friends about this time that she had learnt (in the course of a seance) that in 1911 she would come into a great deal of money.

We are told that there was something sinister about Miss Mountstephen. She specialized in crystal-gazing, and what she saw in the glass often took a violent form. Her 'control', that is her connection in the spirit world, was a dead friend named Mrs Winter.

As a result of their common interest in the occult, Miss

Garnett-Orme took on the younger woman as a companion when she returned to Lucknow in the winter. There they had settled down together. But the summers were spent at one of the various hill stations. Was there a latent lesbianism in their relationship? It was a restless, rootless life, but they were held together by the strong and heady influence of the seance table and the crystal ball. Miss Garnett-Orme's indifferent health also made her dependent on the younger woman.

In the summer of 1911, the couple went up to Mussoorie, probably the most frivolous of hill stations, where 'seasonal' love affairs were almost the order of the day. They took rooms in the Savoy. Electricity had yet to reach Mussoorie, and it was still the age of candelabras and gas-lit streets. Every house had a grand piano. If you didn't go out to a ball, you sang or danced at home. But Miss Garnett-Orme's spiritual pursuits took precedence over these more mundane entertainments. Towards the end of the 'season' on 12 September, Miss Mountstephen returned to Lucknow to pack up their household for a move to Jhansi, where they planned to spend the winter.

On the morning of 19 September, while Miss Mountstephen was still away, Miss Garnett-Orme was found dead in her bed. The door was locked from the inside. On her bedside table was a glass. She was positioned on the bed as though laid out by a nurse or undertaker.

Because of these puzzling circumstances, Major Birdwood of the Indian Medical Service (who was the civil surgeon in Mussoorie) was called in. He decided to hold an autopsy. It was discovered that Miss Garnett-Orme had been poisoned with prussic acid.

Prussic acid is a quick-acting poison, and would have killed too quickly for the victim to have composed herself in the way she was found. An ayah told the police that she had seen someone (she could not tell whether it was a man or a woman) slipping away through the large skylight and escaping over the roof.

Hill stations are hotbeds of rumour and intrigue, and of course the gossips had a field day. Miss Garnett-Orme suffered from dyspepsia and was always dosing herself from a large bottle of sodium bicarbonate, which was regularly refilled. It was alleged that the bottle had been tampered with, and an unknown white powder had been added. Her doctor was questioned thoroughly. They even questioned a touring mind reader, Mr Alfred Capper, who claimed that Miss Mountstephen had hurried from a room rather than have her mind read!

After several weeks the police arrested Miss Mountstephen. Although she had a convincing alibi (due to her absence in Jhansi) the police sought to prove that some kind of sinister influence had been exerted on Miss Garnett-Orme to take her medicine at a particular time. Thus, through suggestion, the murderer could kill and yet be away at the time of death. In Agatha Christie's first novel, *The Mysterious Affair at Styles*, the poisoner was in a distant place by the time her victim reached the fatal dose, the poison having precipitated to the bottom of the mixture. Perhaps Miss Christie had read accounts of the Garnett-Orme case in the British press. Even the motive was similar.

But there was no Hercule Poirot in Mussoorie, and in court this theory could never be made convincing. The police case was never strong (they would have done better to have followed the ayah's lead), and it appears that they only acted because there was considerable ill-feeling in Mussoorie against Miss Mountstephen.

When the trial came up at Allahabad in March 1912 it caused a sensation. Murder by remote control was something new in the annals of crime. But after hearing many days of evidence about the ladies' way of life, about crystal-grazing and premonitions of death, the court found Miss Mountstephen innocent. The chief justice in delivering his verdict, remarked that the true circumstances of Miss Garnett-Orme's death would probably never be known. And he was right.

Miss Mountstephen applied for probate of her friend's will.

But the Garnett-Orme family in England sent out her brother, Mr Hunter Garnett-Orme, to contest it. The case went in favour of Mr Garnett-Orme. The district judge, W. D. Burkitt, turned down Miss Mountstephen's application on grounds of 'fraud and undue influence in connection with spiritualism and crystal-gazing'. She made an appeal at the Allahabad High Court, but the lower court's decision was upheld.

Miss Mountstephen returned to England. We do not know her state of mind, but if she was innocent, she must have been a deeply embittered woman. Miss Garnett-Orme's doctor lost his flourishing practice in Mussoorie and left the country too. There were rumours that he and Miss Mountstephen had conspired to get hold of Miss Garnett-Orme's considerable fortune.

There was one more puzzling feature of the case. Mr Charles Jackson, a painter friend of many of those involved, had died suddenly, apparently of cholera, two months after Miss Garnett-Orme's mysterious death. The police took an interest in his sudden demise. When he was exhumed on 23 December, the body was found to be in a perfect state of preservation. He had died of arsenic poisoning.

Murder or suicide? This puzzle, too, was never resolved. Was there a connection with Miss Garnett-Orme's death? That too we shall never know. Had Conan Doyle taken up Kipling's suggestion and involved himself in the case (as he had done in so many others in England), perhaps the outcome would have been different.

As it is, we can only make our own conjectures.

KIPLING'S SIMLA

Every March, when the rhododendrons stain the slopes crimson with their blooms, a sturdy little steam engine goes huffing and puffing through the 103 tunnels between Kalka and Simla. This is probably the most picturesque and romantic way of approaching the hill station although the journey by road is much quicker.

The train journeys taken to Simla stand out in my memory—the little restaurant at Barog, just before we get to Dharampur, where the roads for Sanawar and Kasauli branch off; and the gorge at Tara Devi, opening out to give the weary traveller the splendid and uplifting panorama of the city of Simla straddling the side of the mountain.

In Rudyard Kipling's time (in the 1870s and 80s), travellers spent the night at Kalka and then covered the sixty-odd hill miles by tonga, a rugged and exhausting journey. It was especially hard on invalids who had travelled long distances to recuperate in the cool clear air of the mountains.

In his story 'The Other Man' (*Plain Tales from the Hills*), Kipling describes the unhappy results of the tonga ride on one such visitor.

> Sitting on the back seat, very square and firm, with one hand on the awning stanchion and the wet pouring off his hat and moustache, was the Other Man—dead. The sixty-mile uphill jolt had been too much for his valve, I suppose. The tonga-driver said, 'This Sahib died two stages out of Solan. Therefore, I tied him with a rope, lest he should fall

out by the way, and so we came to Simla. Will the Sahib give me bakshish?' 'It,' pointing to the Other Man, 'should have given one rupee.'

Today's visitor to Simla need have no qualms about the journey by road, which is swift and painless (provided you drive carefully), but the coolies at the Simla bus stand will be found to be as adamant as Kipling's tonga driver in claiming their baksheesh.

Simla is worth a visit at any time of the year, even during the monsoon. The monsoon season is one of the most beautiful times of the year in the Himalayas, with the mist trailing up the valleys, and the hill slopes, a lush green, thick with ferns and wild flowers. The call of the kastura, or whistling thrush, can be heard in every glen, while the barbet cries insistently from the treetops.

Not far from Christ Church is the corner where a great fictional character, Lurgan Sahib, had his shop—Lurgan being the curio dealer who took the young Kim in hand and trained him as a spy. He was based on a real-life character, who had his shop here. Kipling wrote *Kim* a few years after he had left India. His nostalgia for India, and in particular for the hills, come through in his description of Kim's arrival in Simla in the company of the Afghan horse dealer, Mahbub Ali.

> 'A fair land—a most beautiful land is this of Hind—and the land of the Five Rivers is fairer than all,' Kim half chanted. 'Into it I will go again... Once gone, who shall find me? Look, Hajji, is yonder the city of Simla? Allah! What a city!'

They lead their horses below the main road into the lower Simla Bazaar—'the crowded rabbit-warren that climbs up from the valley to the Town Hall at an angle of forty-five!' And together they set off 'through the mysterious dusk, full of the noises of a city below the hillside and the breath of a cool wind in deodar-crowned Jakko, shouldering the stars.'

Shouldering the stars! That is how I always think of Simla—

standing on the Ridge and looking up through the clear air into the vault of the heavens, where the stars seem so much nearer... And they are reflected below, in the myriad lights of the shops and houses.

For those who want a bit of history, Simla came into being at the end of the Anglo-Gurkha War (1814-16), when most of the surrounding district—captured by the Gurkhas during their invasion—was restored to various States; but the land on which Simla stands was retained by the British—'for services rendered!' Lieutenant Rose built the first house, a thatched wooden cottage, in 1819. His successor, Lieutenant Kennedy, built a permanent house in 1822, which survived until it was destroyed in a fire a couple of years ago. In 1827, Lord Amherst spent several months at Kennedy House and from then on Simla grew in favour with the British. Its early history can be read about in more detail in Sir Edward J. Buck's *Simla, Past and Present*, copies of which sometimes turn up in second-hand bookshops.

From 1865, until World War II, Simla was the summer capital of the Government of India. Later, it served as the capital of East Punjab pending the construction of Chandigarh, and today, of course, it is the capital of Himachal Pradesh.

It is not, however, as a capital city that Simla attracts the visitor but as a place of lovely winding walks, magnificent views, and romantic links with the past. Compared to some of our hill stations, it is well looked after; the streets are clean and uncluttered, the old Georgian-style buildings still stand. And the trees are more in evidence than at other hill resorts.

Simla has a special place in my heart. It was there that I went to school, and it was there that my father and I spent our happiest times together.

We stayed on Elysium Hill; took long walks to Kasumpti and around Jakko Hill; sipped milkshakes at Davico's; saw plays at the Gaiety Theatre (happily still in existence); fed the monkeys at the temple on Jakko; picnicked in Chota Simla. All this during the short summer break when my father (on leave from the Air Force) came up to see me. He told me stories of phantom rickshaws and enchanted forests and planted in me the seeds of my writing career. I was only ten when he died. But he had already passed on to me his love for the hills. And even after I had finished school and grown to manhood, I was to return to the hills again and again—to Simla and Mussoorie, Himachal and Garhwal—because once the mountains are in your blood, there is no escape. Simla beckons. I must return. And, like Kim, I will take the last bend near Summer Hill and look up and exclaim: 'Ah! What a city!'

*

'Romance brought up the nine-fifteen', wrote Kipling and there is still romance to be found on trains and at lonely stations. Small wayside stations have always fascinated me. Manned sometimes by just one or two men, and often situated in the middle of a damp subtropical forest, or clinging to the mountainside on the way to Simla or Darjeeling, these little stations are, for me, outposts of romance, lonely symbols of the spirit that led a certain kind of pioneer to lay tracks into the remote corners of the earth.

Recently I was at such a wayside stop, on a line that went through the terai forests near the foothills of the Himalayas. At about ten at night, the khilasi, or station watchman, lit his kerosene lamp and started walking up the track into the jungle. He was a Gujjar, and his true vocation was herding buffaloes, but the breaking up of his tribe had led him into this strange new occupation.

'Where are you going?' I asked.

'To see if the tunnel is clear,' he said. 'The mail train comes in twenty minutes.'

So I went with him, a furlong or two along the tracks, through a deep cutting which led to the tunnel. Every night, the khilasi walked through the dark tunnel, and then stood outside to wave his lamp to the oncoming train as a signal that the track was clear. If the engine driver did not see the lamp, he stopped the train. It always slowed down near the cutting.

Having inspected the tunnel, we stood outside, waiting for the train. It seemed a long time coming. There was no moon, and the dense forest seemed to be trying to crowd us into the narrow cutting. The sounds of the forest came to us on the night wind—the belling of a sambar, the cry of a fox, told us that perhaps a tiger or a leopard was on the prowl. There were strange nocturnal bird and insect sounds; and then silence.

The khilasi stood outside the tunnel, trimming his lamp, listening to the faint sounds of the jungle—sounds which only he, a Gujjar who had grown up on the fringe of the forest, could identify and understand. Something made him stand very still for a few moments, peering into the darkness, and I could sense that everything was not as it should be.

'There is something in the tunnel,' he said. I could hear nothing at first; but then there came a regular sawing sound, just like the sound of someone sawing through the branch of a tree. 'Baghera!' whispered the khilasi. He had said enough to enable me to recognize the sound—that of a leopard trying to find its mate.

I thought how fortunate we were that it had not been there when we walked through the tunnel. A leopard is unpredictable. But so is a khilasi.

'The train will be coming soon,' he whispered urgently. 'We must drive the animal out of the tunnel, or it will be killed.'

He must have sensed my astonishment, because he said, 'Do not worry, sahib. I know this leopard well. We have seen each other many times. He has a weakness for stray dogs and goats, but he will not harm us.'

He gave me his small hand-axe to hold, and, raising his lamp high, started walking into the tunnel, shouting at the top of his voice to try and scare away the animal. I followed close behind him.

We had gone about twenty yards into the tunnel when the light from the khilasi's lamp fell on the leopard, who was crouching between the tracks, only about fifteen feet away from us. He was not a big leopard, but he was lithe and sinewy. Baring his teeth in a snarl, he went down on his belly, tail twitching, and I felt sure he was going to spring.

The khilasi and I both shouted together. Our voices rang and echoed through the tunnel. And the frightened leopard, uncertain of how many human beings were in there with him, turned swiftly and disappeared into the darkness.

As we returned to the tunnel entrance, the rails began to hum and we knew the train was coming. I put my hand on one of the rails and felt its tremor. And then the engine came around the bend, hissing at us, scattering sparks into the darkness, defying the jungle as it roared through the steep sides of the cutting. It charged straight at the tunnel, and into it, thundering past us like some beautiful dragon from my childhood dreams. And when it had gone the silence returned, and the forest breathed again. Only the rails still trembled with the passing of the train.

As they tremble now to the passing of my own train, rushing through the night with its complement of precious humans, while somewhere at a lonely cutting in the foothills, a small thin man, who must always remain a firefly to these travelling thousands, lights up the darkness for steam engines and panthers. And yet, for the khilasi himself, the incident I have recalled was not an adventure; it was a duty, a job of work, an everyday incident.

For me, all are significant—the lighted compartment, with its farmers, shopkeepers, artisans, clerks and occasional pickpockets; and the lonely wayside stop, with its uncorrupted lamplighter.

Romance still rides the nine-fifteen.

GRANDFATHER'S EARTHQUAKE

'If ever there's a calamity,' Grandmother used to say, 'it will find Grandfather in his bath.' Grandfather loved his bath—which he took in a large, round aluminium tub. He sometimes spent as long as an hour in the tub, 'wallowing' as he called it, and splashing around like a boy.

He was in his bath during the earthquake that convulsed Bengal and Assam on 12 June 1897—an earthquake so severe that even today the region of the great Brahmaputra River basin hasn't settled down. Not long ago it was reported that the entire Shillong Plateau had moved an appreciable distance away from the Brahmaputra towards the Bay of Bengal. According to the Geological Survey of India, this shift has been taking place gradually over almost a hundred years.

Had Grandfather been alive, he would have added one more clipping to his scrapbook on the earthquake. The clipping goes in anyway, because the scrapbook is now with his children. More than newspaper accounts of the disaster, it was Grandfather's own letters and memoirs that made the earthquake seem recent and vivid; for he, along with Grandmother and two of their children (one of them my father), was living in Shillong, then a picturesque little hill station in Assam, when the earth shook and the mountains heaved.

As I have mentioned, Grandfather was in his bath, splashing about, and did not hear the first rumbling. But Grandmother was in the garden, hanging out or taking in the washing (she could never remember which) when, suddenly, the animals began making a hideous noise—a sure intimation of a natural disaster, for animals sense the approach of an earthquake much more quickly than humans.

The crows all took wing, wheeling wildly overhead and cawing loudly. The chickens flapped in circles, as if they were being chased. Two dogs sitting on the veranda suddenly jumped up and ran out with their tails between their legs. Within half a minute of her noticing the noise made by the animals, Grandmother heard a rattling, rumbling noise, like the approach of a train.

The noise increased for about a minute, and then there was the first trembling of the ground. The animals by this time all seemed to have gone mad. Treetops lashed backwards and forwards, doors banged and windows shook, and Grandmother swore later that the house actually swayed in front of her. She had difficulty standing straight, though this could have been due more to the trembling of her knees than to the trembling of the ground.

The first shock lasted for about a minute and a half. 'I was in my tub having a bath,' Grandfather wrote for posterity, 'which for the first time in the last two months I had taken in the afternoon instead of in the morning. My wife and children and the ayah were downstairs. Then the shock came, accompanied by a loud rumbling sound under the earth and a quaking which increased in intensity every second. It was like putting so many shells in a basket, and shaking them up with a rapid sifting motion from side to side.

'At first I did not realize what it was that caused my tub to sway about and the water to splash. I rose up, and found the earth heaving, while the washstand, basin, ewer, cups and glasses danced and rocked about in the most hideous fashion. I rushed to the inner door to open it and search for my wife and children, but could not move the dratted door as boxes, furniture and plaster had come up against it. The back door was the only way of escape. I managed to burst it open, and, thank God, was able to get out. Sections of the thatched roof had slithered down on the four sides like a pack of cards and blocked all the exits and entrances.

'With only a towel wrapped around my waist, I ran out into the open to the front of the house, but found only my wife there. The whole front of the house was blocked by the fallen section of thatch from the roof. Through this I broke my way under the iron railings and extricated the others. The bearer had pluckily borne the weight of the whole thatched roof section on his back as it had slithered down, and in this way saved the ayah and children from being crushed beneath it.'

After the main shock of the earthquake had passed, minor shocks took place at regular intervals of five minutes or so, all through the night. But during that first shake-up the town of Shillong was reduced to ruin and rubble. Everything made of masonry was brought to the ground. Government House, the post office, the jail, all tumbled down. When the jail fell, the prisoners, instead of making their escape, sat huddled on the road waiting for the superintendent to come to their aid.

Wrote a young girl in a newspaper called *The Englishman*, 'The ground began to heave and shake. I stayed on my bicycle for a second, and then fell off and got up and tried to run, staggering about from side to side of the road. To my left I saw great clouds of dust, which I afterwards discovered to be houses falling and the earth slipping from the sides of the hills. To my right I saw the small dam at the end of the lake torn asunder and the water rushing out, the wooden bridge across the lake break in two and the sides of the lake falling in; and at my feet the ground cracking and opening. I was wild with fear and didn't know which way to turn.'

The lake rose up like a mountain, and then totally disappeared, leaving only a swamp of red mud. Not a house was left standing. People were rushing about, wives looking for husbands, parents looking for children, not knowing whether their loved ones were alive or dead. A crowd of people had collected on the cricket ground, which was considered the safest place; but Grandfather and the family took shelter in a small shop on the road outside his house. The shop was a rickety wooden structure, which had always looked as though it would fall down in a strong wind. But it withstood the earthquake.

And then the rain came, and it poured. This was extraordinary, because before the earthquake there wasn't a cloud to be seen; but, five minutes after the shock, Shillong was enveloped in cloud and mist. The shock was felt for more than a hundred miles on the Assam–Bengal Railway. A train was overturned at Shamshernagar; another was derailed at Mantolla. Over a thousand people lost their lives in the Cherrapunji Hills, and in other areas, too, the death toll was heavy.

The Brahmaputra burst its banks and many cultivators were drowned in the flood. A tiger was found drowned. And in North Bhagalpur, where the earthquake started, two elephants sat down in the bazaar and refused to get up until the following morning.

Over a hundred men who were at work in Shillong's government printing press were caught in the building when it collapsed, and, though the men of a Gurkha regiment did splendid rescue work, only a few were brought out alive. One of those killed in Shillong was Mr McCabe, a British official. Grandfather described the ruins of Mr McCabe's house: 'Here a bedpost, there a sword, a broken desk or chair, a bit of torn carpet, a well-known hat with its Indian Civil Service colours, battered books, all speaking reminiscences of the man we mourn.'

While most houses collapsed where they stood, Government House, it seems, 'fell backwards'. The church was a mass of red stones in ugly disorder. The organ was a tortured wreck.

A few days later, the family and other refugees were making their way to Calcutta to stay with friends or relatives. It was a slow, tedious journey, with many interruptions, for the roads and railway lines had been badly damaged and passengers had often to be transported in trolleys. Grandfather was rather struck by the stoicism displayed by an assistant engineer. At one station a telegram was handed to the engineer informing him that his bungalow had been destroyed. 'Beastly nuisance,' he observed with an aggrieved air. 'I've seen it cave in during a storm, but this is the first time it has played me such a trick on account of an earthquake.'

The family got to Calcutta to find the inhabitants of the capital in a panic; for they too had felt the quake and were expecting it to recur. The damage in Calcutta was slight compared to the devastation elsewhere, but nerves were on edge, and people slept in the open or in carriages. Cracks and fissures had appeared in a number of old buildings, and Grandfather was among the many who were worried at the proposal to fire a salute of sixty guns on Jubilee Day (the Diamond Jubilee of Queen Victoria); they felt the gunfire would bring down a number of shaky buildings. Obviously, Grandfather did not wish to be caught in his bath a second time. However, Queen Victoria was not to be deprived of her salute. The guns were duly fired, and Calcutta remained standing.

VOTING AT BARLOWGANJ

I am standing under the deodars, waiting for a taxi. Devilal, one of the candidates in the civic election, is offering free rides to all his supporters, to ensure that they get to the polls in time. I have assured him that I prefer walking but he does not believe me; he fears that I will settle down with a bottle of beer rather than walk the two miles to the Barlowganj polling station to cast my vote. He has gone to the extent of engaging a taxi for the day just to make certain of lingerers like me. He assures me that he is not using unfair means—most of the other candidates are doing the same thing.

It is a cloudy day, promising rain, so I decide I will wait for the taxi. It has been plying since 6 a.m., and now it is ten o'clock. It will continue plying up and down the hill till 4 p.m. and by that time it will have cost Devilal over a hundred rupees.

Here it comes. The driver—like most of our taxi drivers, a Sikh—sees me standing at the gate, screeches to a sudden stop, and opens the door. I am about to get in when I notice that the windscreen carries a sticker displaying the Congress symbol of the cow and calf. Devilal is an Independent, and has adopted a cock bird as his symbol.

'Is this Devilal's taxi?' I ask.

'No, it's the Congress taxi,' says the driver.

'I'm sorry,' I say. 'I don't know the Congress candidate.'

'That's all right,' he says agreeably; he isn't a local man and has no interest in the outcome of the election. 'Devilal's taxi will be along any minute now.'

He moves off, looking for the Congress voters on whose behalf he has been engaged. I am glad that the candidates have had to adopt different symbols; it has saved me the embarrassment of turning up in a Congress taxi, only to vote for an Independent. But the real reason for using symbols is to help illiterate voters know whom they are voting for when it comes to putting their papers in the ballot box. All through the hill station's mini-election campaign, posters have been displaying candidates' symbols—a car, a radio, a cock bird, a tiger, a lamp—and the narrow, winding roads resound to the cries of children who are paid to shout, 'Vote for the Radio!' or 'Vote for the Cock!'

Presently my taxi arrives. It is already full, having picked up others on the way, and I have to squeeze in at the back with a stout lalain and her bony husband, the local ration shop owner. Sitting up front, near the driver, is Vinod, a poor, ragged, happy-go-lucky youth, who contrives to turn up wherever I happen to be, and frequently involves himself in my activities. He gives me a namaste and a wide grin.

'What are you doing here?' I ask him.

'Same as you, Bond sahib. Voting. Maybe Devilal will give me a job if he wins.'

'But you already have a job. I thought you were the games-boy at the school.'

'That was last month, Bond sahib.'

'They kicked you out?'

'They asked me to leave.'

The taxi gathers speed as it moves smoothly down the winding hill road. The driver is in a hurry; the more trips he makes, the more money he collects. We swerve around sharp corners, and every time the lalain's chubby hands, covered with heavy bangles and rings, clutch at me for support. She and her husband are voting for Devilal because they belong to the same caste; Vinod is voting for him in the hope of getting a job; I am voting for him because I like the man. I find him simple, courteous and ready to listen to complaints about drains, street lighting and wrongly assessed taxes. He even tries to do something about these things. He is a tall, cadaverous man, with paan-stained teeth; no Nixon, Heath or Indira Gandhi; but he knows that Barlowganj folk care little for appearances.

Barlowganj is a small ward (one of four in the hill station of Mussoorie); it has about a thousand voters. An election campaign has, therefore, to be conducted on a person-to-person basis. There is no point in haranguing a crowd at a street corner; it would be a very small crowd. The only way to canvass support is to visit each voter's house and plead one's cause personally. This means making a lot of promises with a perfectly straight face.

The bazaar and village of Barlowganj crouch in a vale on the way down the mountain to Dehra. The houses on either side of the road are nearly all English-looking, most of them built before the turn of the century. The bazaar is Indian, charming and quite prosperous—tailors sit cross-legged before their sewing machines, turning out blazers and tight trousers for the well-to-do students who attend the many public schools that still thrive here; potbellied halwais spend all day sitting on their haunches in front of giant frying pans; and coolies carry huge loads of timber or cement or grain up the steep hill paths.

Who was Barlow, and how did the village get his name? A search through old guides and gazetteers has given me no clue. Perhaps he was a revenue superintendent or a surveyor, who came striding up from the plains in the 1830s to build a hunting lodge in this pleasantly wooded vale. That was how most hill stations began. The police station, the little Church of the Resurrection, and the ruined brewery were among the earliest buildings in Barlowganj.

The brewery is a mound of rubble, but the road that came into existence to serve the needs of the old Crown Brewery is the one that now serves our taxi. Buckle and Co.'s 'Bullock Train' was the chief means of transport in the old days. Sir

Henry Bohle, one of the pioneers of brewing in India, started the Old Brewery at Mussoorie in 1830. Two years later he got into trouble with the authorities for supplying beer to soldiers without permission; he had to move elsewhere.

But the great days of the brewery business really began in 1876, when everyone suddenly acclaimed a much-improved brew. The source was traced to Vat 42 in Whymper's Crown Brewery (the one whose ruins we are now passing), and the beer was retasted and retested until the diminishing level of the barrel revealed the perfectly brewed remains of a soldier who had been reported missing some months previously. He had evidently fallen into the vat and been drowned and, unknown to himself, had given the Barlowganj beer trade a real fillip. Apocryphal though this story may sound, I have it on the authority of the owner of the now defunct *Mafasalite Press* who, in a short account of Mussoorie, wrote that 'meat was thereafter recognized as the missing component and was scrupulously added till more modern, and less cannibalistic, means were discovered to satiate the froth-blower'.

Recently, confirmation came from an old India hand now living in London. He wrote to me reminiscing of early days in the hill station and had this to say:

> Uncle Georgie Forster was working for the Crown Brewery when a coolie fell in. Coolies were employed to remove scum etc. from the vats. They walked along planks suspended over the vats. Poor devil must have slipped and fallen in. Uncle often told us about the incident and there was no doubt that the beer tasted very good.

What with soldiers and coolies falling into the vats with seeming regularity, one wonders whether there may have been more to these accidents than met the eye. I have a nagging suspicion that Whymper and Buckle may have been the Burke and Hare of Mussoorie's beer industry.

But no beer is made in Mussoorie today, and Devilal probably regrets the passing of the breweries as much as I do. Only the walls of the breweries remain, and these are several feet thick. The roofs and girders must have been removed for use in other buildings. Moss and sorrel grow in the old walls, and wild cats live in dark corners protected from rain and wind.

We have taken the sharpest curves and steepest gradients, and now our taxi moves smoothly along a fairly level road which might pass for a country lane in England were it not for the clumps of bamboo on either side.

A mist has come up the valley to settle over Barlowganj, and out of the mist looms an imposing mansion, Sikander Hall, which is still owned and occupied by the Skinners, descendants of Colonel James Skinner who raised a body of Irregular Horse for the Marathas. This was absorbed by the East India Company's forces in 1803. The cavalry regiment is still known as Skinner's Horse, but of course it is a tank regiment now. Skinner's troops called him 'Sikander' (a corruption of both Skinner and Alexander), and that is the name his property bears. The Skinners who live here now, quite sensibly, keep pigs and poultry.

The next house belongs to the Raja of K. but he is unable to maintain it on his diminishing privy purse, and it has been rented out as an ashram for members of a saffron-robed sect who would rather meditate in the hills than in the plains. There was a time when it was only the sahibs and rajas who could afford to spend the entire 'season' in Mussoorie. The new rich are the industrialists and maharishis. The coolies and rickshaw pullers are no better off than when I was a boy in Mussoorie. They still carry or pull the same heavy loads, for the same pittance, and seldom attain the age of forty. Only their clientele has changed.

One more gate, and here is Colonel Powell in his khaki bush shirt and trousers, a uniform that never varies with the seasons. He is an old shikari; has written a book called *Call of the Tiger*. He is too old for hunting now, but likes to yarn with me when we meet on the road. His wife has gone home to England, but he does not want to leave India.

'It's the mountains,' he was telling me the other day. 'Once the mountains are in your blood, there is no escape. You have to come back again and again. I don't think I'd like to die anywhere else.'

Today there is no time to stop and chat. The taxi driver, with a vigorous blowing of his horn, takes the car around the last bend, and then through the village and narrow bazaar of Barlowganj, stopping about a hundred yards from the polling station.

There is a festive air about Barlowganj today, I have never seen so many people in the bazaar. Bunting, in the form of rival posters and leaflets, is strung across the street. The tea shops are doing a roaring trade. There is much last-minute canvassing, and I have to run the gamut of various candidates and their agents. For the first time I learn the names of some of the candidates. In all, seven men are competing for this seat.

A schoolboy, smartly dressed and speaking English, is the first to accost me. He says: 'Don't vote for Devilal, sir. He's a big crook. Vote for Jatinder! See, sir, that's his symbol—the bow and arrow.'

'I shall certainly think about the bow and arrow,' I tell him politely.

Another agent, a man, approaches, and says, 'I hope you are going to vote for the Congress candidate.'

'I don't know anything about him,' I say.

'That doesn't matter. It's the party you are voting for. Don't forget it's Mrs Gandhi's party.'

Meanwhile, one of Devilal's lieutenants has been keeping a close watch on both Vinod and me, to make sure that we are not seduced by rival propaganda. I give the man a reassuring smile and stride purposefully towards the polling station, which has been set up in the municipal schoolhouse. Policemen stand at the entrance, to make sure that no one approaches the voters once they have entered the precincts.

Voting at Barlowganj

I join the patient queue of voters. Everyone is in good humour, and there is no breaking of the line; these are not film stars we have come to see. Vinod is in another line, and proudly grins at me across the passageway. This is the one day in his life on which he has been made to feel really important. And he *is*. In a small constituency like Barlowganj, every vote counts.

Most of my fellow voters are poor people. Local issues mean something to them, affect their daily living. The more affluent can buy their way out of trouble, can pay for small conveniences; few of them bother to come to the polls. But for the 'common man'—the shopkeeper, clerk, teacher, domestic servant, milkman, mule driver—this is a big day. The man he is voting for has promised him something, and the voter means to take the successful candidate up on his promise. Not for another five years will the same fuss be made over the local cobblers, tailors and laundrymen. Their votes are indeed precious.

And now it is my turn to vote. I confirm my name, address and roll number. I am down on the list as 'Rusking Bound', but I let it pass: I might forfeit my right to vote if I raise any objection at this stage! A dab of marking-ink is placed on my forefinger—this is so that I do not come around a second time—and I am given a paper displaying the names and symbols of all the candidates. I am then directed to the privacy of a small booth, where I place the official rubber stamp against Devilal's name. This done, I fold the paper in four and slip it into the ballot box.

All has gone smoothly. Vinod is waiting for me outside. So is Devilal.

'Did you vote for me?' asks Devilal.

It is my eyes that he is looking at, not my lips, when I reply in the affirmative. He is a shrewd man, with many years' experience in seeing through bluff. He is pleased with my reply, beams at me, and directs me to the waiting taxi.

Vinod and I get in together, and soon we are on the road again, being driven swiftly homewards up the winding hill road.

Vinod is looking pleased with himself; rather smug, in fact. 'You did vote for Devilal?' I ask him. 'The symbol of the cock bird?'

He shakes his head, keeping his eyes on the road. 'No, the cow,' he says.

'You ass!' I exclaim. 'Devilal's symbol was the cock, not the cow!'

'I know,' he says, 'but I like the cow better.'

I subside into silence. It is a good thing no one else in the taxi has been paying any attention to our conversation. It would be a pity to see Vinod turned out of Devilal's taxi and made to walk the remaining mile to the top of the hill. After all, it will be another five years before he gets another free taxi ride.

A MAGIC OIL

One cosy summer morning in Fosterganj, when not much was happening, but life was going on just the same, I was in the bank, run by Vishaal (manager), Negi (cashier), and Suresh (peon). I was sitting opposite Vishaal, who was at his desk, on which there were two handsome paperweights but no papers. Suresh had brought me a cup of tea from the tea shop across the road. There was just one customer in the bank, Hassan, who was making a deposit.

In walked Foster. He'd made an attempt at shaving, but appeared to have given up at a crucial stage, because now he looked like a wasted cricketer finally on his way out. The effect was enhanced by the fact that he was wearing flannel trousers that had once been white but were now greenish yellow; the previous monsoon was to blame. He had found an old tie, and this was strung around his neck or rather his unbuttoned shirt collar. The said shirt had seen many summers and winters in Fosterganj, and was frayed at the cuffs. Even so, Foster looked quite spry, as compared to when I had last seen him.

'Come in, come in!' said Vishaal, always polite to his customers, even those who had no savings. 'How is your gladioli farm?'

'Coming up nicely,' said Foster. 'I'm growing potatoes too.'

'Very nice. But watch out for the porcupines, they love potatoes.'

'Shot one last night. Cut my hands getting the quills out. But porcupine meat is great. I'll send you some the next time I shoot one.'

'Well, keep some ammunition for the leopard. We've got to get it before it kills someone else.'

'It won't be around for two or three weeks. They keep moving, do leopards. He'll circle the mountain, then be back in these parts. But that's not what I came to see you about, Mr Vishaal. I was hoping for a small loan.'

'Small loan, big loan, that's what we are here for. In what way can we help you, sir?'

'I want to start a chicken farm.'

'Most original.'

'There's a great shortage of eggs in Mussoorie. The hotels want eggs, the schools want eggs, the restaurants want eggs. And they have to get them from Rajpur or Dehradun.'

'Hassan has a few hens,' I put in.

'Only enough for home consumption. I'm thinking in terms of hundreds of eggs—and broiler chickens for the table. I want to make Fosterganj the chicken capital of India. It will be like old times, when my ancestor planted the first potatoes here, brought all the way from Scotland!'

'I thought they came from Ireland,' I said. 'Captain Young, up at Landour.'

'Oh well, we brought other things. Like Scotch whisky.'

'Actually, Irish whisky got here first. Captain Kennedy, up in Simla.' I wasn't Irish, but I was in a combative frame of mind, which is the same as being Irish.

To mollify Foster, I said, 'You did bring the bagpipe.' And when he perked up, I added: 'But the Gurkha is better at playing it.'

This contretemps over, Vishaal got Foster to sign a couple of forms and told him that the loan would be processed in due course and that we'd all celebrate over a bottle of Scotch whisky. Foster left the room with something of a swagger. The prospect of some money coming in—even if it is someone else's—will put any man in an optimistic frame of mind. And for Foster the prospect of losing it was as yet far distant.

I wanted to make a phone call to my bank in Delhi, so that I could have some of my savings sent to me, and Vishaal kindly allowed me to use his phone.

There were only four phones in all of Fosterganj, and there didn't seem to be any necessity for more. The bank had one. So did Dr Bisht. So did Brigadier Bakshi, retired. And there was one in the police station, but it was usually out of order.

The police station, a one-room affair, was manned by a daroga and a constable. If the daroga felt like a nap, the constable took charge. And if the constable took the afternoon off, the daroga would run the place. This worked quite well, as there wasn't much crime in Fosterganj—if you didn't count Foster's illicit still at the bottom of the hill (Scottish hooch, he called the stuff he distilled); or a charming young delinquent called Sunil, who picked pockets for a living (though not in Fosterganj); or the barber who supplemented his income by supplying charas to his agents at some of the boarding schools; or the man who sold the secretions of certain lizards, said to increase sexual potency—except that it was only linseed oil, used for oiling cricket bats.

I found the last mentioned, a man called Rattan Lal, sitting on a stool outside my door when I returned from the bank.

'Saande-ka-tel,' he declared abruptly, holding up a small bottle containing a vitreous yellow fluid. 'Just one application, sahib, and the size and strength of your valuable member will increase dramatically. It will break down doors, should doors be shut on you. No chains will hold it down. You will be as a stallion, rampant in a field full of fillies. Sahib, you will rule the roost! Memsahibs and beautiful women will fall at your feet.'

'It will get me into trouble, for certain,' I demurred. 'It's great stuff, I'm sure. But wasted here in Fosterganj.'

Rattan Lal would not be deterred. 'Sahib, every time you try it, you will notice an increase in dimensions, guaranteed!'

'Like Pinocchio's nose,' I said in English. He looked puzzled. He understood the word 'nose', but had no idea what I meant.

'Naak?' he said. 'No, sahib, you don't rub it on your nose. Here, down between the legs,' and he made as if to give a demonstration. I held a hand up to restrain him.

'There was a boy named Pinocchio in a far-off country,' I explained, switching back to Hindi. 'His nose grew longer every time he told a lie.'

'I tell no lies, sahib. Look, my nose is normal. Rest is very big. You want to see?'

'Another day,' I said.

'Only ten rupees.'

'The bottle or the rest of you?'

'You joke, sahib,' he said, and thrust a bottle into my unwilling hands and removed a ten-rupee note from my shirt pocket; all done very simply.

'I will come after a month and check-up,' he said. 'Next time I will bring the saanda itself! You are in the prime of your life, it will make you a bull among men.' And away he went.

～

The little bottle of oil stood unopened on the bathroom shelf for weeks. I was too scared to use it. It was like the bottle in *Alice's Adventures in Wonderland* with the label DRINK ME.

Alice drank it, and shot up to the ceiling. I wasn't sure I wanted to grow that high.

I did wonder what would happen if I applied some of it to my scalp. Would it stimulate hair growth? Would it stimulate my thought processes? Put an end to writer's block?

Well, I never did find out. One afternoon I heard a clatter in the bathroom and looked in to see a large and sheepish-looking monkey jump out of the window with the bottle.

But to return to Rattan Lal—some hours after I had been sold the aphrodisiac, I was walking up to town to get a newspaper when I met him on his way down.

'Any luck with the magic oil?' I asked.

'All sold out!' he said, beaming with pleasure. 'Ten bottles sold at the Savoy, and six at Hakman's. What a night it's going to be for them.' And he rubbed his hands at the prospect.

'A very busy night,' I said. 'Either that, or they'll be looking for you to get their money back.'

'I'll be back next month. If you are still here, I'll keep another bottle for you. Look there!' He took me by the arm and pointed to a large rock lizard that was sunning itself on the parapet. 'You catch me some of those, and I'll pay you for them. Be my partner. Bring me lizards—not small ones, only big fellows—and I will buy!'

'How do you extract the tel?' I asked.

'Ah, that's a trade secret. But I will show you when you bring me some saandas. Now I must go. My good wife waits for me with impatience.'

And off he went, down the bridle path to Rajpur.

The rock lizard was still on the wall, enjoying its afternoon siesta.

As I wasn't making much as a writer, it did occur to me that I might make a living from breeding rock lizards. Perhaps Vishaal would give me a loan.

THE TAIL OF THE LIZARD

There was a break in the rains, the clouds parted, and the moon appeared—a full moon, bathing the mountains in a pollen-yellow light. Little Fosterganj, straddling the slopes of the Ganga-Yamuna watershed, basked in the moonlight, each lighted dwelling a firefly in the night.

Only Fairy Glen Palace was unlit, brooding in the darkness. I was returning from an evening show at the Rialto in Mussoorie. It had been a long walk, but a lovely one. I stopped outside the palace gate, wondering about its lonely inhabitants and all that might have happened within its walls...

I reached Hassan's bakery around midnight, and mounted the steps to my room. My door was open. It was never locked, as I had absolutely nothing that anyone would want to take away. The typewriter, which I had hired from a shop in Dehradun, was a heavy machine, designed for office use; no one was going to carry it off.

But someone was in my bed.

Fast asleep. Snoring peacefully. Not Goldilocks. Nor a bear. I switched on the light, shook the recumbent figure. He started up. It was Sunil. After giving him a beating, the police had let him go.

'Uncle, you frightened me!' he exclaimed.

He called me 'Uncle', although I was only some fifteen or sixteen years older than him. Call a tiger 'Uncle' and he won't harm you; or so the forest dwellers say. Not quite sure how it works out with people approaching middle age. Being addressed as 'Uncle' didn't make me very fond of Sunil.

'I'm the one who should be frightened,' I said. 'A pickpocket in my bed!'

'I don't pick pockets any more, Uncle. I've turned over a new leaf. Don't you know that expression?'

Sunil had studied up to Class 8 in a 'convent school'.

'Well, you can turn out of my bed,' I said. 'And return that watch you took off me before you got into trouble.'

'You lent me the watch, Uncle. Don't you remember? Here!' He held out his arm. 'Take it back.' There were two watches on his wrist; my modest HMT and something far more expensive.

I removed the HMT and returned it to my own wrist.

'Now, can I have my bed back?' I asked.

'There's room for both of us.'

'No, there isn't, it's only a khatiya. It will collapse under our combined weight. But there's this nice easy chair here, and in the morning, when I get up, you can have the bed.'

Reluctantly, Sunil got off the bed and moved over to the cane chair. Perhaps I'd made a mistake. It meant that Sunil would be awake all night, and that he'd want to talk. Nothing can be more irritating than a room companion who talks all night.

I switched off the light and stretched out on the cot. It was a bit wobbly. Perhaps the floor would have been better. Sunil sat in the chair, whistling and singing film songs—something about a red dupatta blowing in the wind, and telephone calls from Rangoon to Dehradun. A romantic soul, Sunil, when he wasn't picking pockets. Did I say there's nothing worse than a companion who talks all night? I was wrong. Even worse is a companion who sings all night.

'You can sing in the morning,' I said. 'When the sun comes out. Now go to sleep.'

There was silence for about two minutes. Then: 'Uncle?'

'What is it?'

'I have to turn over a new leaf.'

'In the morning, Sunil,' I turned over and tried to sleep.

'Uncle, I have a *project*.'

'Well, don't involve me in it.'

'It's all seedha-saadha, and very interesting. You know that old man who sells saande-ka-tel—the oil that doubles your manhood?'

'I haven't tried it. It's an oil taken from a lizard, isn't it?'

'A big lizard.'

'So?'

'Well, he's old now and can't go hunting for these lizards. You can only find them in certain places.'

'Maybe he should retire and do something else, then. Grow marigolds. Their oil is also said to be good for lovers.'

'Not as good as lizard oil.'

'So what's your project?' He was succeeding in keeping me awake. 'Are you going to gather lizards for him?'

'Exactly, Uncle. Why don't you join me?'

⁓

Next morning Sunil elaborated on his scheme. I was to finance the tour. We would trek, or use a bus where there were roads, and visit the wooded heights and rocky slopes above the Bhagirathi River, on its descent from the Gangotri Glacier. We would stay in rest houses, dharamsalas, or small hotels. We would locate those areas where the monitors, or large rock lizards, were plentiful, catch as many as possible and bring them back alive to Fosterganj, where our gracious mentor would reward us to the tune of two hundred rupees per reptile. Sunil and I would share this bonanza.

Although I had idly considered doing something similar, now that I thought about it it didn't seem like it stood any chance of succeeding. But I was bored, and it sounded like it could be fun, even an adventure of sorts, and I would have Sunil as guide, philosopher and friend.

He could be a lovely and happy-go-lucky companion—provided he kept his hands out of other people's pockets and did not sing at night.

Hassan was equally sceptical about the success of the project. For one thing, he did not believe in the magical properties of saande-ka-tel (never having felt the need for it); and, for another, he did not think those lizards would be caught so easily. But he thought it would be a good thing for Sunil, something different from what he was used to doing. The young man might benefit from my 'intellectual' company. And, in the hills, not many folks had money in their pockets.

And so, with the blessings of Hassan, and a modest overdraft from Vishaal, our friendly bank manager, I packed a haversack with essentials (including my favourite ginger biscuits as prepared by Hassan) and set out with Sunil on the old pilgrim road to Tehri and beyond.

Sunil had brought along two large baskets, as receptacles for the lizards when captured. But as he had no intention of carrying them himself—and wisely refrained from asking me to do so—he had brought along a twelve-year-old youth from the bazaar—a squint-eyed, hare-lipped, one-eared character called Buddhoo, whose intelligence and confidence made up for his looks. Buddhoo was to act as our porter and general factotum. On our outward journey he had only to carry the two empty baskets; Sunil hadn't told him what their eventual contents might be.

It was late July, still monsoon time, when we set out on the Tehri road.

In those days it was still a mule-track, meandering over several spurs and ridges, before descending to the big river. It was about forty miles to Tehri. From there we could get a bus, at least up to Pratap Nagar, the old summer capital of the hill state.

෴

That first day on the road was rather trying. I had done a certain amount of walking in the hills, and I was reasonably fit. Sunil, for all his youth, had never walked further than Mussoorie's cinemas or Dehra's railway station, where the pickings for his agile fingers had always been good. Buddhoo, on the other hand, belied his short stature by being so swift of foot that he was constantly leaving us far behind. Every time we rounded a corner, expecting to find him waiting for us, he would be about a hundred yards ahead, never tiring, never resting.

To keep myself going I would sing either Harry Lauder's 'Keep right on to the end of the road,' or Nelson Eddy's 'Tramp, tramp, tramp'.

Tramp, tramp, tramp, along the highway,
Tramp, tramp, tramp, the road is free!
Blazing trails along the byways...

Sunil did not appreciate my singing.

'You don't sing well,' he said. 'Even those mules are getting nervous.' He gestured at a mule-train that was passing us on the narrow path. A couple of mules were trying to break away from the formation.

'Nothing to do with my singing,' I said. 'All they want are those young bamboo shoots coming up on the hillside.'

Sunil asked one of the mule-drivers if he could take a ride on a mule; anything to avoid trudging along the stony path. The mule-driver agreeing, Sunil managed to mount one of the beasts and went cantering down the road, leaving us far behind.

Buddhoo waited for me to catch up. He pointed at a large rock to the side of road, and there, sure enough, resting at ease, basking in the morning sunshine, was an ungainly monitor lizard about the length of my forearm.

'Too small,' said Buddhoo, who seemed to know something about lizards. 'Bigger ones higher up.'

The lizard did not move. It stared at us with a beady eye; a contemptuous sort of stare, almost as if it did not think very highly of humans. I wasn't going to touch it. Its leathery skin looked uninviting; its feet and tail reminded me of a dinosaur; its head was almost serpent like. Who would want to use its body secretions, I wondered. Certainly not if they had seen the creature. But human beings, men especially, will do almost anything to appease their vanity. Tiger's whiskers or saande-ka-tel—anything to improve their sagging manhood.

We did not attempt to catch the lizard. Sunil was supposed to be the expert. And he was already a mile away, enjoying his mule-ride.

An hour later he was sitting on the grassy verge, nursing a sore backside. Riding a mule can take the skin off the backside of an inexperienced rider.

'I'm in pain,' he complained. 'I can't get up.'

'Use saande-ka-tel,' I suggested.

Buddhoo went sauntering up the road, laughing to himself.

'He's mad,' said Sunil.

'That makes three of us, then.'

~

By noon we were hungry. Hassan had provided us with buns and biscuits, but these were soon finished, and we were longing for a real meal. Late afternoon we trudged into Dhanolti, a scenic spot with great views of the snow peaks; but we were in no mood for scenery. Who can eat sunsets? A forest rest house was the only habitation, and had food been available we could have spent the night there. But the caretaker was missing. A large black dog frightened us off.

So on we tramped, three small dots on a big mountain, mere specks, beings of no importance. In creating this world, God showed that he was a Great Mathematician; but in creating man, he got his algebra wrong. Puffed up with self-importance, we are in fact the most dispensable of all his creatures.

On a long journey, the best companion is usually the one who talks the least, and in that way Buddhoo was a comforting presence. But I wanted to know him better.

'How did you lose your ear?' I asked.

'Bear tore it off,' he said, without elaborating.

Brevity is the soul of wit, or so they say.

'Must have been painful,' I ventured.

'Bled a lot.'

'I wouldn't care to meet a bear.'

'Lots of them out here. If you meet one, run downhill. They don't like running downhill.'

'I'll try to remember that,' I said, grateful for his shared wisdom. We trudged on in silence. To the south, the hills were bleak and windswept; to the north, moist and well-forested.

The road ran along the crest of the ridge, and the panorama it afforded, with the mountains striding away in one direction and the valleys with their gleaming rivers snaking their way towards the plains, gave me an immense feeling of freedom. I doubt if Sunil felt the same way. He was preoccupied with tired legs and a sore backside. And for Buddhoo it was a familiar scene.

A brief twilight, and then, suddenly, it grew very dark. No moon; the stars just beginning to appear. We rounded a bend, and a light shone from a kerosene lamp swinging outside a small roadside hut.

It was not the pilgrim season, but the owner of the hut was ready to take in the odd traveller. He was a grizzled old man. Over the years the wind had dug trenches in his cheeks and forehead. A pair of spectacles, full of scratches, almost opaque, balanced on a nose long since broken. He'd lived a hard life. A survivor.

'Have you anything to eat?' demanded Sunil.

'I can make you dal-bhaat,' said the shopkeeper. Dal and rice was the staple diet of the hills; it seldom varied.

'Fine,' I said. 'But first some tea.'

The tea was soon ready, hot and strong, the way I liked it. The meal took some time to prepare, but in the meantime we made ourselves comfortable in a corner of the shop, the owner having said we could spend the night there. It would take us two hours to reach the township of Chamba, he said. Buddhoo concurred. He knew the road.

We had no bedding, but the sleeping area was covered with old sheepskins stitched together, and they looked comfortable enough. Sunil produced a small bottle of rum from his shoulder bag, unscrewed the cap, took a swig, and passed it around. The old man declined. Buddhoo drank a little; so did I. Sunil polished off the rest. His eyes became glassy and unfocused.

'Where did you get it?' I asked.

'Hassan Uncle gave it to me.'

'Hassan doesn't drink—he doesn't keep it, either.'

'Actually, I picked it up in the police station, just before they let me go. Found it in the havildar's coat pocket.'

'Congratulations,' I said. 'He'll be looking forward to seeing you again.'

The dal-bhaat was simple but substantial.

'Could do with some pickle,' grumbled Sunil, and then fell asleep before he could complain any further.

⁂

We were all asleep before long. The sheepskin rug was reasonably comfortable. But we were unaware that it harboured a life of its own—a miniscule but active population of fleas and bugs—dormant when undisturbed, but springing into activity at the proximity of human flesh and blood.

Within an hour of lying down we were wide awake.

When God, the Great Mathematician, discovered that in making man he had overdone things a bit, he created the bedbug to even things out.

Soon I was scratching. Buddhoo was up and scratching. Sunil came out of his stupor and was soon cursing and scratching. The fleas had got into our clothes, the bugs were feasting on our blood. When the world as we know it comes to an end, these will be the ultimate survivors.

Within a short time we were stomping around like Kathakali dancers. There was no relief from the exquisite torture of being seized upon by hundreds of tiny insects thirsting for blood or body fluids.

The tea shop owner was highly amused. He had never seen such a performance—three men cavorting around the room, scratching, yelling, hopping around.

And then it began to rain. We heard the first heavy raindrops pattering a rhythm on the tin roof. They increased in volume, beating against the only window and bouncing off the banana fronds in the little courtyard. We needed no urging. Stripping off our clothes, we dashed outside, naked in the wind and rain, embracing the elements. What relief! We danced in the rain until it stopped, and then, getting back into our clothes with some reluctance, we decided to be on our way, no matter how dark or forbidding the night.

We paid for our meal—or rather, I paid for it, being the only one in funds—and bid goodnight and goodbye to our host. Actually, it was morning, about 2 a.m., but we had no intention of bedding down again; not on those sheepskin rugs.

A half-moon was now riding the sky. The rain had refreshed us. We were no longer hungry. We set out with renewed vigour.

Great lizards, beware!

~

At daybreak we tramped into the little township of Chamba, where Buddhoo proudly pointed out a memorial to soldiers from the area who had fallen fighting in the trenches in France during World War I. His grandfather had been one of them. Young men from the hills had traditionally gone into the army; it was the only way they could support their families; but times were changing, albeit slowly. The towns now had several hopeful college students. If they did not find jobs they could go into politics.

The motor road from Rishikesh passed through Chamba,

and we were able to catch a country bus which deposited us at Pratap Nagar later that day.

Pratap Nagar is not on the map, but it used to be a place of some consequence once upon a time. Back in the days of the old Tehri Raj it had been the raja's summer capital. There had even been a British resident and a tiny European population—just a handful of British officials and their families. But after Independence, the raja no longer had any use for the place. The state had been poor and backward, and over the years he had spent more time in Dehradun and Mussoorie.

We were there purely by accident, having got into the wrong bus at Chamba.

The wrong bus or the wrong train can often result in interesting consequences. It's called the charm of the unexpected.

Not that Pratap Nagar was oozing with charm. A dilapidated palace, an abandoned courthouse, a dispensary without a doctor, a school with a scatter of students and no teachers, and a marketplace selling sad-looking cabbages and cucumbers—these were the sights and chief attractions of the town. But I have always been drawn to decadent, decaying, forgotten places—Fosterganj being one of them—and while Sunil and Buddhoo passed the time chatting to some of the locals at the bus stand—which appeared to be the centre of all activity—I wandered off along the narrow, cobbled lanes until I came to a broken wall.

Passing through a break in the wall I found myself in a small cemetery. It contained a few old graves. The inscriptions had worn away from most of the tombstones, and on others the statuary had been damaged. Obviously no one had been buried there for many years.

In one corner I found a grave that was better preserved than the others, by virtue of the fact that the lettering had been cut into an upright stone rather than a flat slab. It read:

Dr Robert Hutchinson
Physician to His Highness
Died July 13, 1933
of Typhus Fever
May his soul rest in peace.

Typhus fever! I had read all about it in an old medical dictionary published half a century ago by *The Statesman* of Calcutta and passed on to me by a fond aunt. Not to be confused with typhoid, typhus fever is rare today but sometimes occurs in overcrowded, unsanitary conditions and is definitely spread by lice, ticks, fleas, mites and other microorganisms thriving in filthy conditions—such as old sheepskin rugs which have remained unwashed for years.

I began to scratch at the very thought of it.

I remembered more: 'Attacks of melancholia and mania sometimes complicate the condition, which is often fatal.'

Needless to say, I now found myself overcome by a profound feeling of melancholy. No doubt the mania would follow.

I examined the other graves, and found one more victim of typhus fever. There must have been an epidemic. Fortunately for my peace of mind, the only other decipherable epitaph told of a missionary lady who had fallen victim to an earthquake in 1905. Somehow, an earthquake seemed less sinister than a disease brought on by bloodthirsty bugs.

While I was standing there, ruminating on matters of life and death, my companions turned up, and Sunil exclaimed: 'Well done, Uncle, you've already found one!'

I hadn't found anything, being somewhat shortsighted, but Sunil was pointing across to the far wall where a great fat lizard sat basking in the sun.

Its tail was as long as my arm. Its legs were spread sideways, like a goalkeeper's. Its head moved from side to side, and suddenly its tongue shot out and seized a passing dragonfly.

In seconds the beautiful insect was imprisoned in a pair of

strong jaws.

The giant lizard consumed his lunch, then glanced at us standing a few feet away.

'Plenty of fat around that fellow,' observed Sunil. 'Full of that precious oil!'

The lizard let out a croak, as though it had something to say on the matter. But Sunil wasn't listening. He lunged forward and grabbed the lizard by its tail. Miraculously, the tail came away in his hands.

Away went the lizard, minus its tail.

Buddhoo was doubled up with laughter. 'The tail's no use,' he said. 'Nothing in the tail!'

Sunil flung the tail away in disgust.

'Never mind,' I said. 'Catch a lizard by its tail—make a wish, it cannot fail!'

'Is that true?' asked Sunil, who had a superstitious streak.

'Nursery rhyme from Brazil,' I said.

The lizard had disappeared, but a white-bearded patriarch was looking at us from over the wall.

'You need a net,' he said. 'Catching them by hand isn't easy. Too slippery.'

We thanked him for his advice; said we'd go looking for a net.

'Maybe a bedsheet will do,' Sunil said.

The patriarch smiled, stroked his flowing white beard, and asked: 'But what will you do with these lizards? Put them in a zoo?'

'It's their oil we want,' said Sunil, and made a sales pitch for the miraculous properties of saande-ka-tel.

'Oh, that,' said the patriarch, looking amused. 'It will irritate the membranes and cause some inflammation. I know—I'm a nature therapist. All superstition, my friends. You'll get the same effect, even better, with machine oil. Try sewing machine oil. At least it's harmless. Leave the poor lizards alone.'

And the barefoot mendicant hitched up his dhoti, gave us a friendly wave, and disappeared in the monsoon mist.

STRYCHNINE IN THE COGNAC

Sick was she on Thursday,
Dead was she on Friday,
Glad was Tom on Saturday night
To bury his wife on Sunday.

Miss Bean was reclining in a cane chair in a corner of the hotel's Beer Garden, reciting old nursery rhymes to herself, when Mr Lobo, the resident pianist, walked over and placed a glass of lemon juice beside her.

'Oranges and lemons,' he said, sitting down beside her. 'Which do you prefer?'

'Both,' she said. 'Oranges for the complexion, lemons for the digestion.'

'Words of wisdom. But that nursery rhyme sounded a bit wicked. I can only remember the innocent ones like Jack and Jill.'

'Not so innocent. "Jack fell down and broke his crown"—he wouldn't have survived a broken head. Maybe Jill pushed him over a cliff—and went tumbling after!'

'Like the judge who fell into the Kempty Waterfall. Was he pushed, or did he fall?'

'We shall never know. No witnesses. But here come the Roys—what a handsome couple!'

The Roys were, indeed, a handsome couple, as you would expect them to be. Dilip Roy was in his mid-forties, but still a name to be reckoned with in Bollywood. He was greying a little at the temples, just below the edges of his wig; but he remained lean and athletic looking, and the meaty, romantic roles still came his way. His wife, Rosie Roy, was two or three years younger than him, but inclined to plumpness. When she was in her later twenties and early thirties she had starred in several very popular films—two of them opposite Dilip Roy, whom she had married while on location with him in Kashmir—but of late she had been having some difficulty in getting parts to her liking. She hadn't been feeling very well and had taken to sleeping late in the mornings. Her doctor had suspected diabetes and had advised a complete check-up, but she kept putting off the necessary tests.

'You need change,' said Dilip, always concerned about her health. 'A change from Bombay. A fortnight in the hills will do wonders for you. I'll spend a few days with you too, before I start shooting in Switzerland. Where would you like to go—Simla, Mussoorie, Darjeeling, Ooty?'

'Why not Switzerland?'

Dilip laughed uneasily. 'It wouldn't be much of a holiday. I'd be shooting all the time and you'd be pestered by hangers-on and loads of admirers.'

'Former admirers.'

'Well, better an old admirer than none at all. And I'm still jealous.'

They settled on Mussoorie—partly because Dilip Roy's father was an old friend of Nandu, the owner of the hotel, and partly because Rosie had spent an idyllic summer there as a girl, staying with an aunt in Barlowganj. When the couple arrived at the hotel, the first person they encountered was Miss Bean, watering the potted aspidistras in the porch of the hotel.

'Hello,' said Rosie, smiling curiously at Miss Bean. 'Are you the new gardener?'

'I'm the old gardener,' said Miss Bean. 'A long-time resident, actually. But the gardener never waters these aspidistras—he thinks they are hardy enough to go without. But plants are like humans—they need a little attention from time to time, otherwise they die of neglect. I've seen you somewhere, haven't I?'

'Only if you go to the movies,' said Rosie. And added: 'Old movies.'

'You're Rosie Roy,' said Miss Bean. 'I saw you in *Cobra Lady*.'

'Wasn't it terrible?'

'It was so bad that I enjoyed every moment of it. And this must be the great Dilip Roy,' observed Miss Bean, as the well-known actor joined them, followed by room boys loaded with luggage. 'The hero of *Love in Kathmandu*,' said Miss Bean, but the hero ignored her.

Dilip Roy did not stop to gossip, but continued up the steps to the lobby, followed by his wife and the room boys. Miss Bean gave her attention to the aspidistras.

'Friendly heroine but not so friendly hero,' she said to the nearest potted plant. The aspidistra appeared to agree.

∽

The couple settled in, and over the next few days Miss Bean saw quite a lot of them although she took care not to intrude in any way, for it was obvious that the Roys were not looking for company.

In the evenings Dilip Roy would plant himself on a bar stool, and work his way through several whiskies, occasionally answering polite questions from the bartender or a casual customer, but always rather morosely, his mind obviously elsewhere. In the background, Mr Lobo, the hotel pianist, would play popular numbers but without receiving any encouragement or applause.

Rosie did not join her husband in the bar. But occasionally a Martini was served to her in her room—sometimes two Martinis—it was obvious that she liked a gin and vermouth cocktail now and then. Nandu presented her with a bottle of cognac, and she kept it on her dresser, intending to open it only when her husband was in the mood to drink with her.

They went out for quiet walks together, avoiding the Mall

where they would quickly be recognized by both locals and visitors. Sometimes they passed Miss Bean, who was herself a great walker. As they were fellow residents of the hotel they would stop to exchange comments on the weather, the view, the hotel, the town, sometimes even the country and the rest of the world. But from the quiet of the mountains the rest of the world can seem very far away.

Rosie Roy liked the look of Miss Bean and was always ready to stop and talk. Dilip Roy was polite but brusque. The local gossip did not interest him, and he thought Miss Bean a rather quaint and rather foolish bit of flotsam surviving from the days of the British Raj. But then (as Rosie argued) the hotel, the cottages, the winding footpaths, the hill station itself, were all survivors of the Raj, and if their old-world atmosphere did not please you, it might have been better to holiday in Goa—and soak up the Portuguese atmosphere!

India would always be haunted by its history...

～

One day the Roys had a violent quarrel. Miss Bean was no eavesdropper but she couldn't help overhearing every word that was spoken. Her favourite place was a bench situated behind a tall hibiscus hedge. It looked out upon the snows, and Miss Bean liked to spend a half hour there with a book while Fluff, her little terrier, investigated the hillside, looking for rats' holes. You couldn't see the bench from the Beer Garden, and it was in the Beer Garden that Rosie and Dilip Roy were confronting each other.

'You're off, because of that woman in Bandra.' Rosie's voice was quite shrill. 'A week away from her and you're beginning to look like a real Majnu—all pale and melancholy.'

'Don't make up things.' Dilip Roy sounded impatient rather than melancholy. 'You know they start shooting on the new film next week. And it's in Switzerland, not Bandra.'

'You're not the star. They can do without you. You've been getting too fat for leading roles. And you're drinking too much.'

'I'll end up an alcoholic if I stay here much longer. The doctors advised rest for you, not for me. You've given yourself ulcers and you won't get any better if you worry over trifles.'

Here the couple were interrupted by a group of youngsters seeking autographs, and Miss Bean took advantage of the diversion to slip away, taking a roundabout path to her room. Fluff enjoyed the extended walk.

That evening Dilip Roy opened the bottle of cognac. He was leaving the next morning, and he was in a mood to celebrate. But he was not particularly fond of cognac, and did most of his celebrating with his favourite Scotch. Rosie poured herself a glass of cognac, then put the bottle away on the dresser in their room. There it remained all night.

Dilip Roy breakfasted alone in the dining room, then sent for a taxi to take him down to Dehradun. Rosie did not see him off.

'She's sleeping late,' explained Dilip. 'She has a headache. Don't disturb her.'

'Enjoy yourself in Switzerland,' said Nandu, the affable proprietor.

'Look after Rosie,' said Dilip Roy. 'Let her get plenty of rest.'

And everyone did their best to make Rosie comfortable and welcome, because she was much the more gracious of the two. The manager and staff fussed over her, and Mr Lobo played her favourite tunes, especially the one she always requested:

The future is hard to see,
Whatever will be will be...

Even Miss Bean was drawn towards Rosie and joined her on an inspection of the garden, for they were both fond of flowers, and in late summer the grounds were awash with bright yellow marigolds, petunias, larkspur and climbing roses. They had coffee together and Rosie recalled her parents and happy childhood days spent in Mussoorie; she did not talk about her marriage.

As evening came on, Rosie would retire to her room and send for a Martini; it would be followed by a second. She would have a light supper in her room—usually a chicken or mushroom soup with toast—followed by a few sips of cognac as a nightcap... and then to bed.

This routine continued for three or four days, and the cognac bottle was still half full because Rosie preferred Martinis. Dilip Roy made a couple of calls from Bombay—the crew would be off to Switzerland any day, and meanwhile they were shooting some scenes in Lonavala.

He had been away for almost a week when Rosie suddenly fell ill. At about ten o'clock after her dinner she rang her bell. A room boy answered her summons, found her on her bed, still dressed, and having a fit of sorts. He ran for the manager.

The manager hurried to the room, followed by a concerned Mr Lobo. They found her still having convulsions.

'I'll go get Dr Bisht,' said Lobo, and hurried from the room. Minutes later they heard the splutter of his scooter as he took the winding driveway down to the Mall. Dr Bisht had a scooter too—it was the Age of the Scooter—and he arrived in time to give Rosie some basic first aid and arrange for her to be taken to the local hospital. He was cautious in his diagnosis. 'Looks like food poisoning,' he said, and then his eye fell on the open bottle of cognac, of which about half remained. There was still some liquor in a glass, and he sniffed at it and made a face. 'Or something else... We'd better have this bottle examined.' But that would take time.

A call was put through to Dilip Roy's studio in Bombay; but the actor was in Switzerland, and air flights were not very frequent those days. It would be two or three days before he could return.

Miss Bean visited Rosie Roy every day, and so, occasionally, did Nandu and Mr Lobo. To everyone's relief and amazement,

Rosie made a good recovery. There were crystals of strychnine at the bottom of that bottle, but they had only just begun to dissolve. Another evening's drinking and Rosie would have reached the fatal dose lying in wait for her. For it was obvious that someone had placed the poison in the bottle, and that someone could only have been Dilip Roy, before he had left Mussoorie. Far away at the time of his wife's expiry, he would have the perfect alibi.

Of course, nothing could be proven—all was surmise and conjecture—but Rosie was certain in her own mind that her husband had intended to do away with her in absentia, so to speak—and had very nearly succeeded.

She and Miss Bean had become fast friends, and Rosie found herself confiding all her fears and suspicions to the older person, and turning to her for advice and guidance.

❦

They sat together on the lawns of the Savoy, Rosie reclining in an easy chair, Miss Bean quite at ease on a wooden bench. From indoors came the tinkle of a piano as Mr Lobo played 'September Song'. Miss Bean sang the words softly, almost to herself:

But it's a long time from May to December,
And the days grown short when we reach September.

'That's a pretty song,' said Rosie. 'A little sad, though.'

'September is a sad month,' said Miss Bean musingly. 'The end of summer, the end of all those lovely picnics. Holding hands and paddling in mountain streams. Hot sunny days. And then all that rain—weeks of endless rain and mist. September brings back the sunshine if only for a short time, and then those icy winds will start coming down from the snows.'

'How romantic!' exclaimed Rosie. 'You are lucky to have lived here most of your life. Well, perhaps I'll come and join you when I've finished with that wretched husband of mine in Bombay.'

'What do you intend to do, my dear? Put arsenic in his vodka?'

'Arsenic is too slow. But if he eats enough of those chocolate-coated hazelnuts of which he is so fond, he could well come to a sticky end.'

'What do you mean, dear?'

'This is only for your ears, Auntie May.'

She addressed Miss Bean by her first name whenever she became trustful and confiding. 'I know you won't give me away—just in case something happens.'

'What could happen now?'

'Well, during the last two years I've been so miserable that I've always kept a little cyanide pill with me, just so that I can put an end to my life if it becomes too unbearable.'

'Oh, dear. Do throw it away. Don't even think of doing away with yourself.'

'Well, actually I did throw it away—got rid of it. I took the pill and gave it a nice coating of chocolate and then mixed it up with all the little hazelnut chocolates in the tin that Dilip always carries around.'

'Oh, but that was wicked of you. Quite diabolical! Understandable though, when you think of what he tried to do to you. But he could get to that chocolate pill any day. Pop it into his mouth, and then—'

'Pop off?' added Rosie, a glint in her hazel eyes.

'But it's been some time, hasn't it? Almost three weeks since he left. Someone else might have helped himself or herself to a chocolate—'

Just then they saw Nandu advancing across the lawn. It wasn't his usual amble, he looked very purposeful.

'Bad news,' he said, when he reached their sunny corner. 'I've just had a call from Dilip's manager. Your husband died last night. Suicide, it appears. Cyanide. He must have been feeling very guilty about what happened to you. I'm sorry for your loss, Rosie...'

That evening Miss Bean dined with Rosie in the old ballroom. It was the end of the season, and only a few tables were occupied. Mr Lobo was at the piano, playing nostalgic numbers.

'What will you have, Auntie May? You're my special guest today. It's not that I want to celebrate or anything like that—'

'I quite understand, my dear.'

'So you must have a decent wine, instead of that dreadful crème-de-menthe you make in your room. Here's the wine list.'

Miss Bean ran her eye down the wine list. She was no blackmailer, but she couldn't help feeling a little surge of power as she made her choice. And it was such a long time since she'd enjoyed a really good wine. So she plumped for the most expensive wine on the list, and sat back in anticipation.

WHEN THE CLOCK STRIKES THIRTEEN

Tick-tock,
Tick-tock.

One day that clock will strike thirteen and I'll be liberated for ever, thought Rani Ma as the clock struck twelve and she poured herself another generous peg from the vodka bottle. Recently she had moved from gin to vodka, the latter seemed a little more suited to her mid-morning depression. The bottle was half empty but it would take her through to late afternoon when her ancient manservant, Bahadur, would arrive with another bottle and some vegetables for the evening meal. She did not bother with breakfast or lunch, and yet she was fat, fifty, and oh so forlorn.

Living alone on the seventh floor of a new apartment building—Ranipur's only skyscraper—had only emphasized Rani Ma's loneliness and isolation. Friends had drifted away over the years. Her selfish nature and acerbic tongue had destroyed many relationships. There were no children, for marriage had passed her by. Occasionally a nephew or cousin would turn up, hoping for a loan, but would go away disappointed.

Rani Ma had nothing to live for, and almost every day, after the third vodka, she contemplated suicide. If only that clock would strike thirteen, Time for her would stop, and she would take that fatal leap into oblivion. Because it had to be a leap—something dramatic, something final. No sleeping tablets for her, no overdose of Alprax, no Hyoscine in her vodka. And she was far too clumsy to try slitting her own wrists, she'd only make a mess of it, and Bahadur would find her bleeding on the carpet and run for a doctor. There was an old shotgun in the bottom drawer of a cupboard but the box of cartridges that went with it looked damp and mouldy; of no use, except perhaps to frighten off an intruder. No, there was only one thing to do—leap off her seventh floor balcony, stay airborne for a few seconds, and then—oblivion!

Why wait for that clock to strike thirteen? Time would never stop—not for her, not for all those thousands below, hurrying about in a heat of hope, striving to find some meaning in their lives, some sustenance for their hordes of children; some happy, some miserable but alive...

She opened the door to her balcony and stood there, unsteady, supporting herself against the low railing. Down below on the busy street, cars, scooters, cyclists, pedestrians, went about their business unaware of the woman looking down upon them from her balcony. Once the queen of Ranipur, she had always looked down upon them. Now her rule extended no further than her apartment, and the world went by unheeding.

Tick-tock, tick-tock, why keep listening to that wretched clock? Time must have a stop.

∽

Walking along the pavement with a jaunty air, hat at an angle, humming an old tune, was Colonel Jolly, recently retired. He was on his way to the bank to collect his pension, and he enjoyed walking into town, nodding or waving to acquaintances, stopping occasionally to buy a paper or an ice cream, for he was still a boy as far as ice creams went. He was enjoying his retirement; his sons were settled abroad, his wife was at home baking a cake for his evening tea. He was in love with life and he hadn't a care in the world.

As he passed below the tall apartment building, something came between him and the sun, blocking out his vision. He had no idea what it was that struck him, bringing about a total eclipse. One moment he was striding along, at peace with the world; the next, he was flat on the pavement, buried beneath a mountain of flesh that had struck him like a comet.

Both the Colonel and Rani Ma were rushed to the nearest hospital. The Colonel's neck and spine had been shattered and he died without recovering consciousness. Rani Ma took some time to recover; but, thanks to her fall, having been cushioned by the poor Colonel, recover she did, retiring to a farmhouse on the outskirts of town.

Colonel Jolly, lover of life, had lost his to a cruel blow of fate. Rani Ma, who hated living, survived into a grumpy old age.

She is still waiting for the clock to strike thirteen.

THE HORSESHOE

'What's this?' asked Rakesh, when he was a small boy, touching the huge horseshoe that stood on my desk.

'It's a horseshoe,' I said, 'I keep it for luck.'

'But it's so big! It must have been a very big horse. Like a dinosaur!'

'Not a dinosaur, but an English carthorse. They are not very tall, but they are sturdy animals, used to pull carts and ploughs. And they have big feet. This is a carthorse's shoe. About four times bigger than the shoes of the little hill ponies we see in Mussoorie.'

'Are there any carthorses in India?'

'Not as far as I know. You'll find them on farms in England or France.'

'Then how did you get it, Dada?'

'Miss Bean gave it to me.'

And then I told him about Miss Bean, the old English lady who had grown up in Mussoorie, and who lived in Maplewood Cottage when I came to live there in 1963.

Yes, it's exactly fifty years since I came to live in the hill station, renting the little cottage that stood on its own on the edge of a maple and oak forest. Rakesh wasn't born then.

Miss Bean was in her eighties, the 'last surviving Bean' as she described herself. Her parents, brother and sister were all buried in the Camel's Back Cemetery. She received a tiny pension and lived in a small room full of bric-a-brac, bits of furniture rescued from her old home, and paintings done by her late mother. I was on my own then, living on sardines, baked beans and other tinned stuff. Sometimes I shared my simple meals with her.

She told me stories of Mussoorie's early days—the balls and fancy dress parties at Hakman's and the Savoy; the scandals that erupted from time to time; houses that were said to be haunted; friends who had gone away or gone to their Maker; her father's military exploits.

I had noticed the big horseshoe on the mantelpiece, and asked her how she came by it. 'My father brought it out from England,' she said. 'It was supposed to bring us luck. But the good luck ran out long ago... You can have it, if you like it.' And she presented me with the horseshoe.

Well, it's been with me all these years, going almost unnoticed most of the time, except when a visitor notices it and comments on its size.

Miss Bean passed away in her sleep, while I was still at Maplewood. Prem came to work for me, and brought his wife and three-month old Rakesh from the village to live with us. They stayed for the rest of my long sojourn in the hills.

Rakesh is now forty. He and his pretty wife Beena have three school-going children. The horseshoe is still reclining on my desk.

Beena was asking me about it this morning. 'Did it really bring you good luck?'

'We make our own luck,' I said. 'But that horseshoe has been with us all these years, and it always reminds me of its former owner, a little old lady who didn't have much luck, but who enjoyed living and stood alone, without complaining. It's courage, not luck that takes us through to the end of the road.'

ACKNOWLEDGEMENTS

Almost all my early stories, novellas and essays made their first appearance in different periodicals and anthologies, both Indian and international. I would like to acknowledge these publications in the order in which the stories in this book are published. If a piece is appearing in the book for the first time I have not mentioned it in the acknowledgements below.

'The Big Race': *The Road to the Bazaar*, Rupa Publications; 'Up the Spiral Staircase': the *Christian Science Monitor*; 'A Long Walk for Bina': *A Long Walk for Bina*, Rupa Publications; 'When the Guavas are Ripe': *The Road to the Bazaar*, Rupa Publications; 'The Night Train at Deoli': *The Night Train at Deoli and Other Stories*, Penguin India; 'The Visitor': *The Road to the Bazaar*, Rupa Publications; 'Of Rivers and Pilgrims': the *Christian Science Monitor*; 'A Good Place for Trees': *School Magazine*, N. S. W., Australia; 'Time Stops at Shamli': *Dust on the Mountain*, Penguin India; 'Bus Stop, Pipalnagar': *The Night Train at Deoli and Other Stories*, Penguin India; 'The Funeral', 'Some Hill Station Ghosts': *Roads to Mussoorie*, Rupa Publications; 'A Hill Station's Vintage Murders': *Strange Men, Strange Places*, Rupa Publications; 'Kipling's Simla': *Strange Men, Strange Places*, Rupa Publications; 'Grandfather's Earthquake': *Strange Men, Strange Places*, Rupa Publications; 'Voting at Barlowganj': *Blackwood's Magazine*; 'A Magic Oil': *Tales of Fosterganj*, Aleph Book Company; 'The Tail of the Lizard': *Tales of Fosterganj*, Aleph Book Company.

R. B.